THE SAGA OF
BJORN UNFRID

John L. Simons Jr.

RINTH PRESS

HOUSTON, TX

Paperback ISBN: 979-8-9889660-5-0

Rinth Press

RinthPress.net

Houston, Texas

Acknowledgements

This little book had the help of many hands and I'd like to thank them all. Thanks to my critique group, Sherry Ballantine, Kai Haggerty, Marva Mason, Corrie Peters, and Amber Zade. My editor T.J. McKay did an amazing job finding the weak points I had to fix and guiding me to a better story. I had great early readers including Stefanie Barnfather, Sasha Fountain, Krissy Krolczyk, TJ List, and Alex Perez. Beth Anderson did an awesome job putting the book together. Huge thanks to Chris Carson for creating a cover that pulled together Houston art themes I never knew existed. Thanks to the University of Houston for welcoming me all those years ago and planting the seeds that would eventually inform this book.

Finally, thanks to Gabino Iglesias for talking to a cabbie about writing. This book would not have happened without that conversation.

1

"The omens say don't go."

Bjorn's mother set his empty teacup back in front of him.

In his heart, Bjorn was caught in the crevice between childhood and adulthood, the place where his mother and father faded from authorities to advisers. Despite wanting to forge his own path, he mourned gently at the diminishment of his parents. He would go, and that choice made him feel callous and disquieted. Yet he would go.

Bjorn poured more tea into the cup and swirled it around. "Now I shall read the tea leaves for myself," he said, and emptied the cup of bitter fluid in a single gulp, swallowing the leaves as well. He showed his mother the clean porcelain bottom of the cup.

"The tea leaves are telling me the way is clear," Bjorn said.

She began to tousle his hair affectionately as she had done when he was small and ran around causing mischief, but then she stopped and held her hands by her side.

"I don't understand why you want to leave Canada so badly." She said, but Bjorn knew she had accepted his decision because she'd spoken in English. Outside of Nordic

1

Canada, no one spoke Norse. Even at the last minute she was preparing him to live among Americans.

"Ég er ekki að fara frá Jarlandi, ég er að fara til Ameríku," Bjorn said in Norse. *I'm not leaving Canada, I'm going to America.*

Reluctantly, Bjorn's mother drove him to Pearson Airport.

When the plane was wheels-up, he couldn't bring himself to look down on Toronto as it receded into his past.

Before the morning was over, Bjorn found himself under a hotter, brighter sun. He took off his *Class of '85* high school sweatshirt and tied it around his waist. The air of the Texas coastal plain was thick with humidity and smelled of baked concrete overlaid by the honey scent of coneflowers.

He took the bus from the airport to the University of Houston where he checked into his room in Settegast Hall, had a late lunch, and went through orientation before selecting classes. He fretted over every class, feeling that each decision shaped his future like molding clay. Was he making a vase or an ashtray? In one day, he changed countries and climate, moved into a new home with a roommate he had never met, and chose the path for his future. Life was careening out of control faster than he had ever experienced...

...until, that is, he stood in line, papers in hand, waiting to be churned through the administrative process.

Bjorn shuffled a step closer. There were maybe 30 people ahead of him when he looked down at the course selection form and noticed the name at the top did not say Bjorn Unfrid. He had spelled it out for his guide three times and it was spelled correctly on his admission paperwork, but his guide had scribbled "Barny Unfriend." Bjorn had expected to bond with his guide over their matching Iron Maiden t-shirts, but his guide had remained cool to him.

Fucking Anglos.

Anglos and Norsemen might have similar skin color, but

Bjorn was keenly aware the cultural contrasts were sharp. His first time visiting a country descended from British colonialism, he felt like everyone was staring at him. Today he stood out for the very things that made him blend in at home. Bjorn was half a head taller than anyone else in the room. His blonde hair hung past his shoulders and his meticulously manicured beard was a cone that came to a perfect point.

Worse for Bjorn were his mismatched blue and brown eyes, which often drew second glances even at home. Did it make him look eccentric to wear wrap-around sunglasses indoors? Yes. Better eccentric than freakish, but he would have preferred not to stand out at all. He hadn't realized until this moment how much he valued anonymity, how comforting it felt to be overlooked in a crowd. He was accustomed to being around indigenous people in Canada, but this place was filled with every hue and size of human from every corner of the Earth. None of them looked like him and it made him feel like all eyes were turned his way as the line slowly progressed.

Bjorn thought he was going to pass out from the heat by the time he arrived at the window and handed his course selections to the clerk. She was a grim woman not much older than he was. Bjorn could go all day in a room of unsmiling people back home, but this was America. Smiling at each other for no reason was a cultural imperative. He decided to give American chattiness a try.

"I'm excited to be here," he said. "I like the campus and I can already tell that everyone is enthusiastic about everything in the United States. It is a little exhausting, but I like it." He curved his lips into a pretend smile. It took as much effort as drawing the ends of a heavy hunting bow, but he did it.

The clerk side-eyed him but did not return the smile. She, for one, did not seem like an enthusiastic American. He decided to try one more time.

3

"I bet your job will be a lot easier when they fix the air conditioning."

The clerk still did not return the smile. "The AC is working perfectly. This is what we keep it set to," she said.

"Jesus Christ!" Bjorn exclaimed. He had almost blurted out *Odin's balls!* but caught himself just in time. His father had taught him to use local profanity when traveling to avoid standing out as a foreigner.

The clerk looked down and scanned his paperwork. Now she seemed chatty. "You came all the way from Toronto for an English degree?" she asked. "Don't you speak English there?" Bjorn could hear the challenge in her tone and see the disapproving look on her face.

"Canada has three official languages, Norse, Ojibwe, and English. I could have pursued English in Canada but I wanted to see the world," Bjorn said. It was true, but it was the least of his reasons for choosing UH. Somehow it seemed too private to admit out loud that he was following a girl. He feared people might misunderstand and assume he was letting lust determine the direction of his life. He didn't want his decisions trivialized that way.

The clerk frowned and narrowed her eyes at him. "Everyone says you have strange customs in Canada. You don't practice witchcraft, do you?" She asked. Americans were notoriously critical of the Old Lore Canada was known for.

"No, I don't practice witchcraft," Bjorn said, "but even if I did, I always heard you have religious freedom here. Is that not true?"

"Of course it is," she said. The clerk adjusted her hair and unobtrusively pulled a pendant from where it was hidden under her shirt. She let it hang in full view. It was an eye surrounded by Gaelic flourishes, an old talisman of protection that was still popular in lands that had once been British colonies. The clerk's face immediately became a dark swirl devoid of features, impenetrable to the rarer spiritual senses. If he had tried to see her past or her future, she would have been an emptiness to him.

"We believe certain people have gifts given to them by the Gods," said Bjorn, "but that's not witchcraft."

"I'm sure it isn't," said the faceless clerk, "we accept everyone no matter what their beliefs are."

"I feel very welcome right this minute," said Bjorn.

"However," she continued, "there is a problem with your paperwork. The admission documents and course selection documents appear to be for two different people."

"No," Bjorn said, "my guide made a spelling mistake. All this paperwork is for me."

"You should have corrected your guide's mistake then. These have to match up. I can't use any of this. It's near the end of the day so you'll have to re-do it and bring it back tomorrow."

"But that will be late registration! I don't know if I'll get my classes! It will only take me two seconds to change it right now!"

The faceless clerk shrugged. "I have other people in line, Mr. Unfriend. You can't make them wait. You'll have to go through late registration."

Bjorn still could not see her face, but he heard the self-satisfied tone in her voice. He wondered if she was smiling at last.

"Odin's balls!" he muttered.

2

"You know, some people –not me, but some people – might consider it creepy the way you stare out the window all the time, you know what I mean? Because it's like you're stalking your prey. Or maybe it's like in a horror movie where the unsuspecting victim visits a haunted house and looks up to see the face of a ghost in the attic window when no one has lived in the house for 30 years. And all the audience is yelling at the victim to run away because we all know the ghost is deranged and dangerous but they don't because they're stupid and it's a horror movie. You're that ghost. And you're kind of haunting all the other students down there."

Bjorn's gaze remained fixed on the window. "Discontented spirits seek to finish something left undone in life. They are rarely violent."

"Okay, I guess that's one viewpoint, although I have to mention that ghosts don't exist. Neither do trolls, goblins, pixies, fairies, demons, vampires, or the Easter Bunny."

"The Easter Bunny is a dirty lie," said Bjorn.

"The point is that I wasn't talking about ghosts really. I know it sounded like I was talking about ghosts because those are the words I was using. But I was talking about you creeping out all the other students who live around us. I'm not concerned with imaginary monsters from movies. I'm concerned about our peers whispering behind your back and calling you the Creep."

"I am not interested in their opinions but thank you for your concern for me."

"You're welcome! But actually I'm the one interested in their opinions. Five days into the semester and '*the Creep*' is how they know you. And do you know what that makes me? That makes me the Creep's roommate."

Bjorn grunted.

"If you haven't figured out where I'm going with this, being the Creep's roommate is the opposite of being cool. And when I say I am concerned about the opinions of our peers, you can substitute the words 'fuckable women' for 'peers.' Yes, I want a good GPA, but getting laid is also a goal for this semester. It's not the one and done kind of goal either. I'd like it to be more of a repeat activity. Being the Creep's roommate means I'll be lucky to get a date with a bottle of hand lotion."

Bjorn removed his sunglasses and turned his face to his roommate. "Kevin of the Armitages," said Bjorn. "Among the young Norse folk of Canada we have a tradition we call the Turning."

"Where you turn into werewolves?"

"The Turning is the summer solstice after high school graduation so it is a turning point of the year, but also where children turn into adults."

"Somebody gives you a plaque or something?"

"No, we gather in a clearing deep in the woods and make a great bonfire. Then we drink alcohol and have sex with as many people as we can until morning."

Kevin stared, his eyes huge. "And your parents are okay with this?"

"Officially no, but everyone knows about it. And then,

when a Norseman or Norsewoman goes to college he or she can focus on grades instead of sex."

"Canada is starting to sound really cool," said Kevin, "but we don't have that here and people are still calling you the Creep, so maybe you could stop staring out the window at them? And I'm not 'Kevin of the Armitages.' It's Kevin Armitage. Or just Kevin. My friends call me Kev. You can call me Kev, if you like. You know, provisionally until we see how things work out between us. Also, you could smile from time to time and maybe blink once in a while. That would go a long way toward getting people to stop calling you the Creep."

Bjorn blinked, then curled his lips back into a smile.

"Nevermind. Forget I suggested that. Just go back to the way you were."

"As you wish, Kev."

Bjorn had already learned a few things about his roommate. Kevin Armitage suffered from the Texas heat almost as much as Bjorn did. He came from a farm in the Midwest with mild summers running through corn rows and pleasant breezes in the shade of apple trees. He was descended from Celts and Germanic barbarians and he worked part-time in a furniture store. Kev was shorter and thicker than Bjorn, had dark hair, and always sat as if whatever chair he was in was a recliner.

While Bjorn looked at his roommate, He suddenly felt a pull, a familiar attraction, a magnetic force that drew his gaze back to the window. A few students walked through the Quad courtyard, but one was ascending the steps to Oberholtzer Hall, the administrative building and cafeteria for the Quad. Oberholtzer was situated in the middle of the four dormitories. The woman wore a sleeveless doe-leather jerkin, jean shorts, and sneakers. Her skin was almost the same soft brown color as her jerkin, and her straight black hair hung down to the backs of her knees. She was as familiar as the neighborhood where he grew up. She had lived in an apartment building owned by her tribe just down the street from the park where Bjorn spent much of his time. She was here, and she lived somewhere in the same dorms. He had heard this was where she went and he had felt it in his heart, but to see her with his own eyes made relief flood through him.

"Anja!" Bjorn said, pushing himself up against the window as if he were in a prison trying to escape his cell.

"Did you finally find your... friend?" asked Kev.

"Yes, but I'm not sure she knows me," he replied.

"Yeah, see Bjorn, that's why they call you the Creep."

3

Professor Linsky was normally late, the last person to enter his classroom, but tonight he was early. As usual, he began by addressing the class with *dobrey vyecher*, but because he didn't need to launch into his lesson to catch up, he chatted with the students for a few minutes first.

His classmates were not like the students in Bjorn's other classes. Because he had registered late, he had to take a night class. The class was small, only nine students. Except for one other student, they were all much older than he was, maybe 10 years or so. The day classes were packed with full time students out of high school, but the night classes were dominated by older students taking continuing education or finally trying to earn their degree a credit at a time after work.

Linsky loosened his tie as he leaned an elbow on the small classroom's podium. A minute later he tightened his tie up again. Bjorn had begun counting each time the professor did this, recording the adjustments in the margins of his notebook.

"What made you take this class?" Linsky asked a woman in the front row.

"It will look good on my resume," she said.

The professor gave her a smile and a wink. "The tests to be hired are very difficult," he said. It sounded to Bjorn like they were talking in code, each understanding the other but not spelling out the details. He looked around at the other students. No one else looked like they were missing the subtext.

"I want to be an analyst. Right now I'm a forensic accountant," the woman said. Linsky gave her an approving lift of his eyebrows and moved on to the next student. All of them wanted Russian for their resumes, except for the other student his age. Her name was Irina and her family came from a town called Irkutsk generations ago, and she wanted to speak Russian with her grandmother before the old woman died.

"And what about you, Barny?" asked Linsky.

"My name is Bjorn. The student roster is wrong."

"You should get that fixed," said the professor. "Why are you in this class?"

"I needed a foreign language credit and went through late registration, so this was the only class still available."

"You could have waited and taken an easy Spanish class next semester," said the professor.

"If babies in Russia can learn to speak Russian, I can too," said Bjorn.

Professor Linsky laughed and started class. They went over the alphabet again. The letters still looked like nonsense to Bjorn, but he repeated what he heard.

When the hour was over, the part-time students gathered their things and rushed out the door. Perhaps they had been away from home all day and still had to eat dinner. Linsky scooped up his books and papers and followed them, leaving Irina and Bjorn alone.

"You live in the Quad?" asked Bjorn.

She nodded. "In Taub."

She was an Honors Program nerd then.

"I'm in Settegast," he said, feeling like he was admitting to being from the wrong side of town. They left the classroom together, stepping into the last few minutes of the lowering sun. A wind rustled through Agnes Arnold Hall, a building with open architecture that replaced hallways with breeze-ways along the outer edges of the building. The stifling heat was almost tolerable.

They both went down two flights of stairs and then walked in the same direction but not together. It seemed awkward to Bjorn, them being together but not being together. This would happen Monday, Wednesday, and Friday for the rest of the semester. That seemed like too much awkwardness even for Bjorn. His only option was to make conversation.

"Did you think it strange that all the other students are studying Russian so they can put it on their resumes?" he asked. "What companies are looking for Russian language skills? Professor Linsky seemed to know, but he didn't say. I felt like I was the only one in the room who didn't know what they were talking about."

"You *were* the only one in the room who didn't know," she said. "They're talking about the CIA. You can't expect people who want to be in the CIA to blurt out what they mean. You need to read the room."

Bjorn laughed. "What, our whole class wants to become spies? That seems far-fetched!"

"It's very hard to conduct business in the Soviet Union," she said, "so there are few companies they could apply to, but the CIA is always looking for Russian-speaking analysts. Reagan's last budget expanded CIA operations. Where do you think they recruit Russian speakers?"

"I never thought about it," he said, turning his head and looking at her. Despite the sun setting behind her dark hair, she seemed to have crossed into a shadow. He looked around. The sun was low, but still mercilessly bright. He looked back at her, subdued by shadows although no shadow was cast upon her. He stopped.

Irina kept walking a few seconds before she stopped and glanced back at him.

Even from behind, she was still touched by darkness while all else was in light.

"Is something wrong?" she asked.

"The Norse people know that one day we will lose Ragnarok and be destroyed along with our gods. We fight knowing our doom. Something is always wrong to a Norseman." he said.

4

Bjorn had cut the legs off three pairs of jeans because he did not own any shorts. Cutoff shorts were fine for going back and forth on campus, but the only jeans he had left were almost new and he could not bear to cut them down as well. He had to buy some more clothes.

Bjorn got up and headed toward the door.

"Where are you going?" asked Kev.

"I need to get some t-shirts and shorts."

"The bookstore has t-shirts and jerseys but they won't have shorts."

"I was going to go off campus."

"Walking?"

Bjorn nodded.

"Campus is in the middle of one of the worst parts of town," said Kev. "The campus police are like a forcefield around the university. Everything is cool as long as you stay on campus. But you shouldn't step off campus if you're on foot."

"I'll take a bus then."

"Seriously? Houston has crappy buses. And like I said, this is not the part of town to be out in public. Just because you're a Viking doesn't make you invincible."

"Norseman," Bjorn corrected. "Vikings are raiders. Not all Norsemen are Vikings."

"Don't you Canadians call criminals Vikings, too?"

"Yeah, because raiding is, you know, illegal. We also call adventurers Vikings. Indiana Jones would be a great Viking."

"You're not Indiana Jones, either. You shouldn't leave campus."

Bjorn left. He couldn't stand the heat and he needed more appropriate clothing even if it meant getting mugged in an alley. And he hadn't been completely forthcoming with Kev. Bjorn was a Norseman, but he came from one of the most notorious Viking families of Toronto. He had seen violence fit for a battlefield. He had just been squeamish about joining the family business up to this point.

And he wanted sandals, too. He dreamed of how cool his feet would be with only the barest of footwear. He must go.

Bjorn soon learned he did not need to worry about being mugged in an alley. Houston was not a city of alleys. It was a driving city, spread out with flowing arteries made of an efficient freeway system. He paralleled the nearby freeway, plodding block after block, crossing luxuriously wide streets. Visibility was excellent, which changed the entire feel of being mugged for Bjorn.

Alleys made petty crime into a matter of ambush. Here it was different. He could see them coming in advance. He passed a gas station and convenience store combo where two young men were hanging out by the ice machine. They fell into step well behind him, strolling with a casual confidence. They had done this before. Bjorn felt better knowing he was dealing with pros. Amateurs were unpredictable.

Bjorn could see three more young men about a block up. He looked around. With them ahead and behind, the trap was closing and there was no escape. He could try to run but he wouldn't get far before the heat sapped his strength and they caught up to him. *This*, he thought, *is how lions hunt*.

Bjorn knew life was risky, but today had been the wrong day to gamble.

Eventually he closed the distance to the three men ahead. He stopped a few feet from them and heard the men behind walk up and stop. The trap had closed.

"Do you mind if I ask you a question?" Bjorn said.

"Bro," said the man in the lead, whose lips came together imperfectly in a lopsided grin under a beefy nose. "I wanted to ask you a question. I was hoping you could help us out. Maybe you could loan me a few bucks."

"Sure," said Bjorn. "But while I was walking I was thinking about this situation. There are very few pedestrians in Houston, and they are going to be people without enough money to have a car. You have to stand around all day in the heat to rob just a few people. So much discomfort for so little return. It seems like a bad business model. Is it profitable? It seems sketchy."

"We're not robbing you. We just want a loan until payday."

"You Anglos all have to pretend you're not doing what you're doing when we all know what's happening."

"Fuckface, my name is Lucio! I'm Columbian, not an Anglo."

Bjorn waved the correction aside. "All the same to me," he said. "You all think like an Anglo. Color of your skin and place you were born don't matter so much. If you were Norse, we would have been done with this already and could go on with our business. The Norse recognize that efficiency is a virtue."

The little gang did not appear to appreciate his critique of their thieving style.

Lucio dropped his grinning demeanor and drew a gun from behind his back. "I don't take shit from fuckheads like you." He turned his head to the man on his left. "Can you believe this guy?"

Since Lucio wasn't paying attention, Bjorn knocked the gun aside and stepped in so he could grab the gang leader at the throat and crotch. He bent his knees to drop his center of gravity below Lucio's. *Lift with your legs*, he thought to himself. Bjorn didn't want to give himself back problems.

"Stop touching my cock!" Lucio shouted.

Then Lucio was in the air. Bjorn pivoted, hurling Lucio into the two men behind him as if throwing a shotput. All three men crashed to the ground. Lucio landed badly on one leg and lay crumpled, rocking back and forth holding his knee. The other two moaned and made feeble attempts to get up. Bjorn turned to the front where the largest of his attackers swung his fist in a devastating haymaker.

The man was almost as tall as Bjorn and more heavily muscled. His haymaker was powerful but slow. Bjorn slid forward inside the blow. He drove his own fist into the man's face, straight and quick using the force of his whole body as he'd been taught. The big man collapsed.

Bjorn had learned to punch from his Uncle Rik after Rik got out of prison. Rik also taught him knives and how to get into a locked car. Uncle Rik was a man with a lot of useful knowledge, and he was happy to share it with the children of his family.

Bjorn turned to the last man standing, who glanced at his companions groaning on the cement.

"Hey," said the man, but he did not make a move.

"Hey," said Bjorn.

"You should get a baseball cap," said the man. "This sun will burn your scalp even through your hair. You got to protect yourself from the sun. Also, drink lots of water."

"Carlos, get that asshole!" screamed Lucio.

"Sure, boss," said Carlos. "I'm just waiting for an opening." Carlos gave Bjorn a nod of the head and a wave.

Bjorn returned the nod and walked a few more blocks, but the heat drained the energy from him. At an intersection, the freeway formed an overpass. In the darkness below the freeway, homeless people huddled to escape the sun. The shade seemed to Bjorn like an alluring oasis.

He crossed the feeder road and entered the shade. He expected it to be cool, but it wasn't. The constant radiation of the sun was no longer a worry, but the overpass held hot unmoving air like a heat bubble. He could at least rest a bit before moving on.

As he sat, Bjorn began to feel nausea in the pit of his stomach.

"I should have brought water," he said to himself, but he soon decided the nausea wasn't from dehydration. The sensation throbbed in waves, each wave stronger than the last. Before long he could tell that the pulses emanated from the left side. He looked in that direction and saw a man sitting a short distance from him. The man was dirty and weathered and wore a brown winter coat despite the heat and sat clutching his knees to his chest. He rocked back and forth mumbling to himself.

As soon as he set eyes on him, Bjorn was drawn in. He could feel the craving greater than hunger, greater than sex, greater than love, an addiction that had twisted a full human being into a desperate, single-minded creature. The walls of the man's mind had been eroded by drugs until there was no barrier to keep other souls out. Bjorn felt as if he had fallen into a pit.

Then Bjorn was in the man's past where lurked memories of a long-ago wife, a daughter, proud parents, a job in car sales that was at once dissatisfying but adequate. But a normal life was not this man's destiny. Strange incidents troubled him. He saw things as parts. Life was disassembly. Objects were not the sum of their parts. The man marveled that his daughter and her left arm were no longer together.

There was a dog and a tail, but not the tail of a dog. Other things changed as well. Light started to be brighter to him. People and things developed halos. Everything glowed. The world was full of luminous objects. There was a sandwich and there was a stove but he could not be certain which was which. One day his chair began speaking to him. Its language was so disrespectful he had to chop it up to silence it. He hid the body parts in bags weighted with rocks and threw them in Lake Conroe. Still, the ghost of the chair spoke to him.

The schizophrenia diagnosis came shortly after that incident. And then the medications. They helped, but made him feel dead inside, robotic. He began to fear that it was all a plot by his wife to control him. She was a clerk at City Hall. They could have told her to do this to him.

He stopped taking his meds and soon lived on the streets. He found street drugs. They did not end his visions or confusion but eased the accompanying anxiety.

Bjorn tore his eyes away and threw up on the concrete. He looked at his hand and wiggled his fingers. They all seemed disconnected. He looked around. Everything was made of separate pieces and nothing fit together to form a whole. He crawled away from the man and slowly things returned to normal. When he stood up again, he was in the middle of a group of half a dozen homeless people. He looked from one to the next. Most of them had minds whose barriers had been chemically ground down the same as the schizophrenic man Bjorn encountered first. He found himself in all their lives. He was an executive who lost his job, house, and family. He was a black man beaten behind a Circle K for making eye contact with a white woman. He was a little girl who could feel her skin tearing as her stepfather jammed his engorged penis into her ass.

Bjorn was nearly run over as he fled the overpass. His body trembled and craved a hit of cocaine. He would take anything though, Speed, tranqs, whisky, whatever. The craving devoured him.

Bjorn had never tried drugs in his life.

By the time the traffic cleared enough for him to cross, he was feeling more composed. He no longer cared about the shorts, t-shirts, and sandals he longed to buy. He didn't care about the heat. He trudged back to his room in Settegast. His scalp felt hot with fever. He had a sunburn through his hair. Carlos had been right; he had to buy a baseball cap.

"Did you get your stuff?" asked Kev.

Bjorn grabbed his cup, went into the bathroom, and turned on the cold water. He gulped three cups of water before answering. "I think you were right," he said. "Walking off campus is not a good idea. Can you drive me to Target later?"

"Sure," said Kev. "We'll raid it like Vikings."

5

Anja had lunch around 11:30 on Monday, Wednesday, and Friday. Bjorn wasn't very hungry at that time, but he went anyway and picked slowly on a chicken leg or a tasteless cheeseburger. He would get a cup of coffee and a sugary, artificial dessert and nurse them until she was done eating. The meal plan was a buffet that at first seemed generous and tasty, but soon revealed itself to be monotonous and difficult to stomach. Bjorn was already eating less than normal.

But food did not concern him much. His real problem was how to talk to Anja. If he approached her and said, "Oh, don't I know you? Are you from Toronto?" It would be awkward because he had not done that the first time he saw her in the cafeteria. If he ignored their shared origin and approached her and they began to spend time together, eventually she would find out where he was from. Then there would be strange questions that might lead to her find out he had known her all along and had chosen to say nothing. Would that not make him seem like the Creep that Kev always talked about?

Bjorn felt like he had painted himself into a corner.

What if she did not feel the connection that he felt? He

didn't know anyone else who was like him. He yearned to speak to her, to share the secrets he knew only Anja would understand.

Bjorn looked away quickly. She sometimes had a companion. The companion had just arrived and seen Bjorn staring. Bjorn was suddenly fascinated with his coffee mug. He gazed into it as Anja's companion walked over and sat in the chair across from him. Bjorn did not lift his eyes.

"You looked at me."

There was no getting out of the situation. Bjorn looked up. Anja's companion was a tall, brown native, hirsute and naked except for moccasins and a loincloth. His head was that of an antlered elk. This was a Manitou, a spirit of the People, sometimes referred to as an Arcana. Such was Anja's power and destiny that this Manitou had followed her far from its home to guard and teach her.

"I didn't mean to look at you," said Bjorn. "I wanted to avoid your attention."

"Yet here we sit. Did you think you could follow a holy woman without being noticed?"

"I understand her major is chemical engineering. It doesn't seem like a holy course of study."

"Humans often wander through the wilderness without taking the straight path," said the Manitou, "but they arrive at their destination in the end."

"What if they just die in the wilderness?" asked Bjorn.

"Then that was their destination."

"Maybe she just wants to be like everyone else."

"She's not. And neither are you."

"I want to be with someone like me."

The Manitou snickered. "Because the two of you are different from others does not make you the same as each other."

"Do you ever talk about these things with her?"

"She does not see me. I come to her in dreams or by whispering in her ear. It is this way for most mortals who have Gifts unless they are close to death. Then the veil falls from their eyes. You have a rare and penetrating sight."

"It's a curse."

"Would you like me to take this Gift from you?" asked the Manitou.

Bjorn tried to say yes, but the word stuck in his throat.

The Manitou cocked its head to the side. "You have accepted what you are, then, but cannot bring yourself to like it."

"I suppose that is true."

"Take comfort that in this regard you are no different from many of the ordinary humans sharing this cafeteria with you. You mortals reject yourselves with the tiniest excuse. Hair color, a few pimples, a nose that's just a bit different. It's astonishing, really."

Bjorn cleared his throat. "Getting back to the topic, can you teach me about this Gift?" asked Bjorn, but the Manitou was gone.

He looked around and found Anja staring at him strangely.

Bjorn blushed and managed an uncomfortable smile. He bussed his table and hurried out of the dining room as if someone had uncovered his deepest thoughts and written them on the wall.

6

Bjorn lay sprawled across his bunk, a marked-up paperback edition of *Hamlet* in his hands, as Kev burst into the room, panting and moist with sweat.

"You have been outside in the sun longer than it takes to walk into an airconditioned building, I see," said Bjorn.

"Yeah, it's hot out," replied Kev, "But I thought it would be good to get some exercise walking around campus."

"Ambitious for a Saturday afternoon. For you anyway. Where did you go?"

"I started with the usuals," said Kev. "I went up and down every floor of the architecture building and laughed at all the architecture students sleeping on the couches because they have to stay there all the time to finish their projects."

"In five years they will be making four times as much money as you," said Bjorn.

"I know. That's why I have to laugh at them while I can."

"And then I guess you just stood around in the sun until you were drenched so you could stink up our room?"

"No, then I went down to the Satellite and had a cup of coffee. The place was unexpectedly crowded and I had to share a table with this dude who turned out to be a theater professor. He was really interesting to talk to. Who knew the profs can be real people when they're not in front of a class? If I had any desire to waste my time with theater classes, I would totally take his play writing class. Professor Albee was cool."

Bjorn looked up from *Hamlet*. "Professor Albee teaches how to write plays? Was this *Edward* Albee, maybe?"

"Yeah, it was! Look at you, getting to know random profs around campus! I told the prof that with his ideas, he should just skip the teaching thing and try to make a go of writing plays for real."

"So glad you told him that," said Bjorn, returning to *Hamlet*. "I'm sure he would never have thought of that himself. Your impact on American theater will be remembered forever."

7

Bjorn did not normally pry into other people's lives, but he usually asked Irina several questions whenever he saw her. As the days grew shorter, the sun hung lower on the horizon as they walked back to the Quad after Russian class. The closer they came to nightfall, the deeper the shroud that clung to her. Sometimes her face was lost to him in the darkness except for the glitter of her eyes. Bjorn wanted to understand this doom that approached her and learn if it was Fate or if it could be averted.

He had not yet found the answer to that question, but he had learned that Irina was not what she appeared to be. She had a quick smile when eyes were on her, but a grim expression when she thought no one was looking. She had become so accustomed to Bjorn that the two of them could walk all the way from Agnes Arnold to Taub without her smiling once. He took it as an honor, an unspoken confidence that she let him see her without the mask she always wore.

"Did you come all this way to get away from your parents?" she asked. Bjorn suspected the question revealed more than it asked.

"No," he said, "I have always felt close to my family. And

I have a huge family! But sometimes I think they have forgotten about me in the crowd. I can imagine my mother waking up in the middle of the night and running to my room to see my empty bed and wondering where I was because she forgot I was gone."

Irina laughed without turning up the corners of her mouth. Bjorn felt a connection to her at that moment.

"My mother always knows where I am," said Irina. "I think she keeps a journal of my movements and gives me a daily grade on how well I do what she has told me to do. Can you believe she tells me how to walk?"

"How many ways are there to walk?" Bjorn asked.

"The most important thing to remember is to not be too sexy when I'm walking, unless I mean to be. She doesn't want me to look slutty, but I should know how to attract a man when I find one who is a good catch."

"What's a good catch?"

"Wealthy family, on a good career track," she said.

"What is he supposed to be like, this superior man?"

"I don't think his personality or thoughts matter much. My mother has never emphasized those things. She divorced my father when he lost his big shot job, so I don't think she cared about anything except his money."

"I think if I were always forced to act a certain way I would do the opposite," said Bjorn. "I would walk like a slut all the time. I would have spike heels and tight skirts."

"Ha! Take a look at this," said Irina in her mirthless laugh. She stopped him on the sidewalk and took a moment to compose herself, then walked forward as if on a tight rope. She seemed suddenly more curvy, her hips rising and falling like the pitch and draw of an ocean's waves. Then she stopped and looked back at Bjorn, one eyebrow arched.

His throat was dry and he had difficulty composing words. "Yeah, I would walk like that all the time if I could."

"I would too if I didn't always forget. I've practiced all the things my mother told me for so long that I don't remember anything else. I don't know who I am without her," said Irina, the arched eyebrow gone, her face dark and grim. "I don't know what I am or what I'm good for."

Bjorn felt Irina let her guard down in a moment of complete openness. It seemed as if he were at the top of a steep hill with Irina at the bottom. He slid toward her, scrabbling for a handhold that he could use to stop moving. But some part of himself was fascinated by her and welcomed the intimacy. He lost his grip and felt like he was falling. The motion ceased and he found himself deep in her soul, an empty, bitter place. She was cold and solitary at her core because that was how she endured.

"You are strong," he said. "That is a good thing."

"People don't want strength," she said. "They want love." She gave him a flirtatious look, but that was just playing at love. Going down that path would only leave her more alone than before.

"What about your parents?" she asked when he did not respond to her flirting. "What do they expect from you? Is it a lot? Is it unbearable? Does it make you want to squeeze your head between your hands and scream? Is it a good conversation starter for a party?"

This wasn't something Bjorn wanted to talk about, but he knew if he wasn't candid with Irina she would know instantly. He didn't want to endanger his newfound rapport with her through pointless secrecy.

"I don't think my parents are as bad as that," he said. "My family has *family* expectations."

"What does that mean?"

"Traditions."

"I see you are Mr. Vague tonight."

"Do you believe in magic?" he asked.

"Is this a Canadian thing?"

"No. Even in the north most people do not believe in

magic. But there is a legend about my family. My great-great-great-grandfather was wounded in a fight. Being a good follower of Odin, a Valkyrie came to take him to Valhalla. But when he saw her, he fell in love and would not go. He insisted she stay with him. She fell in love with this mortal whose love was so great that he refused to die. She stayed with him and they married. Since then our family has always been attuned to the spirit world, and the flying horse of the Valkyrie is our family symbol. We are a family of the sky. Some of us can learn to fly."

Irina stopped again and turned to him, this time both eyebrows raised in skepticism.

"I thought we were becoming friends," she said, "and that you always told me the truth."

"I always tell everyone the truth," said Bjorn. It is a Norse custom, but especially those of us who honor Loki."

"I thought Loki was evil."

"Common misconception. He is mischievous but speaks truth to power."

"If you say so. But you're not serious about your family being able to fly, are you?"

"Let me give you one example. My grandfather fought in World War Two as a paratrooper. He died in the war, but after it was over, some of his brothers in arms came to visit my grandmother. They told her he went on over twenty missions and was always the first one to jump out of the plane. He never had a parachute."

Irina laughed and then covered her mouth with her hand. "I'm sorry," she said, "but don't you think maybe what really happened is that he went out of the plane without a parachute just one time and that's why they were visiting your widowed grandmother?"

Bjorn tried to smile back at her. It was a crooked, forced smile, but he knew it was the kind that Irina could understand and appreciate. "True or not, it's part of the family legend. And I made a pledge. You know, I am a disappointment after my brothers. They are all in the family business, but I am not sure it's for me, so one day I promised that I would go away and not return until I could fly like my grandfather."

He took a deep breath in and held the air. He felt the energy and motion of it, felt the lines of force that streamed from his lungs and into the atmosphere as he exhaled. The air was deceptively powerful but also quixotic. He could sense it, but it would not bend to his will.

"Taking after your grandfather is not so hard," she said. "Anyone can fall out of a plane."

She did not smile at him, but at least she gave him a wink.

8

There were moments when Bjorn knew he was acting like a crazy Norseman, but there was nothing he could do to stop himself.

He raised his hand.

"Yes, Mr. Unfriend."

Bjorn hated history class because people wrote history according to the way they wanted to see it, not necessarily according to the way it happened. It provoked Bjorn's stubborn combativeness.

"The Battle of Detroit was not a Canadian attempt to steal American land. It was a response to breaking the Ohio Accords."

"It's good that you brought this up, Mr. Unfriend, because this shows how small events in history can lead to huge conflicts later. This is the largest point of contention between Canada and the US today," said the professor.

"Global warming, over development of wild lands, fishing on our waters…"

"What was that, Mr. Unfriend?"

"I was just trying to figure out if there was a bigger conflict, but I think you are right."

The professor frowned. "Thank you for your concurrence." Professor Melchow was a broad man in a bad suit. He cut an imposing figure in academics but had more reputation than Bjorn thought he deserved. "But the Ohio Accords were an agreement made when the British first colonized North America and discovered that Nordic people had already been on the continent since Leif Erikson arrived in Newfoundland around the year 1000 AD. The agreement was made between the British Government and the Jarls who spoke for the Northern lands that would later come to be known as Canada in English and Jarland in Norse. After the British colonies won their freedom, the Ohio Accords no longer applied because the government that signed the agreement was no longer on the continent."

"A deal is a deal," said Bjorn.

"The Colonials who lived in the Ohio valley and the Michigan territory held a referendum on which country to join. They voted to be American citizens," said Melchow. "Despite that, Canada sent war parties into Ohio and down into Wisconsin, sparking the Canadian-American War. It is still one of the bloodiest conflicts in American history. Canada holding onto the Upper Peninsula of Michigan is a huge disagreement between the two countries to this day."

"Lower Peninsula of Canada," muttered Bjorn.

"So you see, the people in those territories engaged in self-determination," said Professor Melchow.

"American laws permitting slavery made an easy path to wealth," said Bjorn. "But slavery was outlawed in Canada. The Colonials wanted to keep slavery so they could get rich. Indians in Ohio and Michigan were not notified of the vote. The referendum was crooked. The same thing happened in Texas in the war with Mexico."

"That's true," said a Latino student on the other side of the classroom.

"Are you from Mexico?" Melchow asked the Latino student.

"San Antonio."

"Sounds like you both have juicy material for your term papers," Melchow said. "But keep in mind that the final will be graded based on the facts as presented in this course."

Against his better judgment, Bjorn opened his mouth again. "What sort of grade will I get if I just tell the truth?"

9

The elevator opened and Bjorn stepped out onto the top floor of the library where the rare book collection was stored. It was the library's smallest floor. He imagined it on top of the building like a beanie on someone's head. The room held half a dozen solid wood tables and matching solid wood chairs that looked like they, too, had survived from the distant past.

One other student, a woman in the farthest corner of the smallish room, pored over a ginormous tome and scribbled furiously on a legal pad.

Besides that one tome, there were no books. Opposite the elevator there was a counter with a fiercely acerbic-looking librarian standing on the other side. Bookshelves filled the space behind the librarian, where a patron of the library could not reach them. Bjorn realized the librarian would fetch the desired book and give it to the reader, just like being served a ham on rye across a deli counter.

The librarian demanded Bjorn's library card as he approached.

"First time in the Rare Books Section?" asked the librarian.

Bjorn nodded. "Our English professor told the class we

had to look at an original printing so we could appreciate having a research library like this at our disposal."

"We have rules," said the librarian with a sigh. "First, no pens, just pencils. Second, all books stay here. You can't check them out. Third, you can only handle the books in this section while wearing cotton gloves. That leads us to rule number four: you must return the cotton gloves before you leave."

"That is a lot of rules to look at a book."

"This is not B. Dalton, young man! These books were old when your grandparents were learning to write with crayons, so you have to treat them with far more care than the books you have at home," said the librarian, a single curl of black hair dipping across his forehead.

"You are wrong about that," said Bjorn. "My family is very old. In my house we have a book from the 14th century. It is the story of Johanna Skold. She had a disagreement with her brother because she would not submit to the will of their father and follow her duty to her family. Her brother vowed he would force her to behave so she vowed she never would."

"O-o-o-kay…" said the librarian.

"Then she killed him and ripped out his intestines. The book is a scroll with pictures in the margins. A drawing of the intestines form a border around the text for almost three feet! The historians in the Norse Academy call the drawings marginalia and say they were added in the 18th century, probably by a schoolboy. They say it is also historically significant. Imagine if you or I drew in the margins of one of these books and then a few centuries from now someone called our doodling historically significant."

"Nice story," said the librarian. "I'm going to revise rule number one just for you. You can't have a pencil in here either. Now, which book would you like to read?

"I don't remember."

The librarian closed his eyes. "Then why did you come?"

"It was in Latin. My Latin isn't good so I don't remember."

"Your English teacher sent you to look at a book in Latin?"

"Yeah, I was wondering about that myself, but he says we should see it. I was thinking if it is in Latin you would not have too many and you might know which one it is."

"I don't," said the librarian with a twitch in his eye. "We have a lot of books in Latin."

"How about showing me the most popular Latin book you have then?" asked Bjorn. "Since he sent the whole class, that is probably the correct one."

The librarian cocked his head to the side and gave a dead-eyed look but disappeared into the stacks to return only a minute or two later with a thick, leather-bound volume.

"This book was published in 1737. People have regularly asked for it as long as I've worked here."

Bjorn wiggled his fingers into the proffered cotton gloves and picked up the huge book. A scream startled Bjorn, who whipped his head around to see what had happened. But there was no one there.

"Careful! Careful!" exclaimed the librarian. "What is wrong with you?"

"I'm sorry," said Bjorn. "I thought I heard something." He looked down at the book. He heard a pitiful sobbing come from somewhere nearby. He opened the book to a random page and his vision filled with fire. A murmuring surrounded him as if a crowd pleaded for mercy. His joints ached and he felt a searing pain in his side. A great weight was crushing the bones of his feet and his gums began to bleed.

Bjorn closed the book on the counter and pushed it back across the counter.

"Aren't you going to look at it now that I got it for you?" asked the librarian with an annoyed tone in his voice.

"When a book gets old enough it has more stories than

just the ones written in its pages. But some stories are too painful to read," said Bjorn, already heading for the elevator.

While he waited for the doors to open, he turned to the librarian. "It feels more like a TV night to me."

The librarian curled his lips into a sneer as Bjorn stepped into the elevator. "Maybe you can find a movie adaptation of the book."

"I hope not!" Bjorn said as the doors closed and the elevator returned him to ground level.

10

"I can't believe you're doing me this way," said Kev.

"It's All Hallows Eve," said Bjorn. "It's the only American holiday Canadians wish we had. I have always wanted to dress up in costume."

"You could, you know, just decide to celebrate it in Canada too."

"Then we would have to admit to being jealous of Americans. Our pride is too big for that."

"How about a traditional costume, like maybe a sheet thrown over your head with eyeholes cut in it?"

"What is that?"

"That's a ghost. Haven't you ever seen a ghost?"

"That is not what a ghost looks like."

"Every time you say something like that, it's a trap for me to ask what a question like 'what do ghosts really look like' so you to go off about crazy shit. I'm not biting this time."

Bjorn shrugged.

"Look," said Kev, "You could dress as anything. Why would you go as the one thing that will make this harder on me?"

Bjorn wore a white tube dress with bare shoulders. The

fabric scintillated like Mother of Pearl. He finished the outfit with a string of fake diamonds, elbow-length white gloves, and a pair of stiletto heels. He had frequented a Salvation Army store until he could put the whole ensemble together. He had curled his hair like Madonna in one of her videos and applied lavish makeup that would make a clown envious. He stroked his beard while Kev pleaded.

"Irina invited me to an All Hallows Eve party she is going to," said Bjorn. "This is an inside joke between us. I shall walk like a material girl."

"It's not funny to me."

"I do not see how it affects you at all."

"Your whole Creep reputation has affected my reputation. Nobody wants to come by our room."

"I have enjoyed the solitude."

"I haven't! And I'm not just talking about women, either. Last year some random friend would knock on my door and be like 'hi' and I'd be like 'hey' and they'd be like 'hey' and we would hang out for no reason at all. Now nobody wants to come by, even people I knew before you put a curse on my life."

"Maybe they were not true friends."

"Maybe not, but I used to be popular."

Bjorn looked skeptical but said nothing.

"So I decided that if I can't get away from your reputation, maybe I should lean into it. I went down to the UC and visited the student organizations. I found one called Student Paranormal Association and joined it."

"I thought you did not believe in such things."

"To me it's a social organization," said Kev. "It's no stupider than talking about politics or religion."

"Your cynicism seems worse and worse to me the more I come to know you."

"I'm a pragmatist. People ramble on about the weather or their pets or why Sylvia Plath put her head in an oven and mostly it's just jibber-jabber that doesn't mean anything so I don't care what the subject is most of the time. Anyway, it's a small group and I am the only guy in it, which is the important detail."

"Oh," said Bjorn. "Sounds like you are right where you want to be."

"For once, yeah. And I have been playing up the whole Canadian mysticism thing for them. I started out researching things to share with them but that was a lot of work so then I just made stuff up about Native Americans and Norse gods. Don't act too surprised if they ask you stupid questions. Just roll with it. I hope you don't mind that too much, but even if you do I don't actually care. Anyway, they love it, so for the first time all semester knowing you has improved my standing with a group of women. We are having a special meeting tonight and I promised to introduce you to them. And then you go and wear this get up. You could at least shave your beard and get rid of the clown makeup."

"That is what makes it funny," said Bjorn.

"It's fucking All Hallows Eve! Why can't you dress up as a serial killer like everyone else?"

"I will go to your meeting, Kev, but I won't stay long. And I won't change my costume." Kev was not happy about it, but there was never anything Kev could do to change Bjorn's mind.

They got into Kev's 1972 blue Nova and Kev turned it on.

"You should take this thing to a mechanic."

"It has always sounded like this."

"That makes the need even more urgent," said Bjorn.

Kev drove them to a nearby off-campus house rented by the two founders of the Paranormal Student Association. It was in the dilapidated and crime-ridden area that surrounded the campus. For safety, Kev always drove to the Association meetings even though the house was only a few blocks away. The house had been built in the 1940s and was run down but not falling apart. The day ebbed and darkness descended on the city. A pair of evilly grinning jack-o'lanterns flanked the front door, candles casting a flickering light from their eyes and gaping mouths. Kev rang the doorbell.

The door opened and a curvy woman in a blood-spattered cocktail dress stood before them. "Nice dress, Mary," said Kev.

"I'm Bloody Mary. Get it?" asked the woman. "Also, we have actual Bloody Marys to drink. Is this your roommate?"

"Yeah, this is Bjorn," Kev said. He sounded deflated.

"Heterochromia," Mary said.

"What?" asked Kev.

"He has a blue eye and a brown eye. It's called hete-rochromia when you have eyes that don't match. Some people believe it's a sign that a person possesses mystical powers. I love it!"

"It's a genetic condition," said Bjorn. "Some of my family have it too."

Two other women came up behind Mary. One wore tattered clothes and had grey skin. Perhaps she was a zombie. The other wore a furry shirt and gloves. She was probably a werewolf. Kev introduced them as Connie and Sharon.

"You take the paranormal seriously," said Bjorn. He would have to remember their names by the costumes they wore because all three girls had faces obscured by black swirls. He could see no protective amulets, so someone placed hexes by hand. It was hard to do properly if learned from a book, so it had probably been taught, handed down through family in one of the old Traditions. "One of you has a grandmother or grandfather who had the Sight, maybe was a Shaman," said Bjorn.

"Me," said Mary. "Do you read minds?"

"It's a party trick," said Bjorn, "a probable guess. Every-thing is math."

"Yeah, he knows his crowd," said Kev. "What are the chances one of you wouldn't have a mystic in the family?"

"Bjorn, your dress is nicer than any of mine," said Sharon.

"Thanks."

"Not a very scary costume," said Connie.

"In Canada we are afraid of American cultural colonialism."

"He's joking," said Kev. "It takes a long time to get his sense of humor. Until then he just seems like a weird asshole, but he's not." Kev smiled and tried to look like he believed what he said.

"Everyone expects Canadians to be different," said Mary with a laugh.

A fourth woman walked up behind the other three. She was almost as tall as Bjorn and draped in red and black robes. Bjorn could not tell what the costume was because she, too, was obscured from his sight, but under a different kind of protection. Almost her entire form was blanked out, and the blackness did not swirl like a wispy dark cloud. Instead, it was like looking at a wall of knots made of ebony cables. It was a power Bjorn had never seen, perhaps forgotten lore.

"And who is this?" he asked with a nod to the newcomer.

The three girls looked behind them, then back at him.

"Jesus!" said Connie. "You spooky bastard! You had me there for a second."

"Don't do that!" said Mary.

"It was kind of funny," said Sharon. "Kev, I like his sense of humor! For a moment I thought he saw a ghost."

"Ha to the ha," said Kev.

A chill went down Bjorn's spine. No one else could see the fourth woman.

There was always risk in making contact in the spirit realms, but Bjorn opened his senses. The figure became no clearer, but he perceived a membrane in front of him across the door, a spiritual demarcation of some kind.

"Have you done a summoning?" he asked.

"No," said Mary.

"You've done something," Bjorn said.

"The only thing we've done is consecrate the house for protection."

"Consecrate it to what?"

"We just consecrated it in general. Holy places are protected."

"A consecrated place is always consecrated to something," Bjorn said, "And not everything is there to protect you."

"You're doing your weird shit again," said Kev. "Can we just take it inside for the moment? We're letting the mosquitos in."

Bjorn glanced at the robed figure behind the three women, then put his hand on Kev's shoulder. "I cannot stay," he said. "I have a prior party to go to. Kev, you are welcome to accompany me. Come with. Please." Bjorn did not want to leave Kev with the unknown spirit.

Kev looked pissed. "I just got here. I'm not leaving because you need a ride to your party."

Bjorn was afraid of that.

He considered Thor and Loki. Loki meant moral courage, and Bjorn wasn't sure Loki was up to supplying as much as Kev might need. Thor meant power. Bjorn lifted his hand from Kev's shoulder and poked his roommate in the forehead. He flicked his finger back and forth in a few quick movements. Kev flinched and swatted his hand away. Bjorn had traced the rune of Thor on Kev's forehead. He could see the symbol in his roommate's aura but he had done a shitty job. Runes of protection were not one of his strengths.

"Fuck off!" said Kev.

"Be safe," said Bjorn, who turned and walked away in his stilettos, tripping as he went.

Connie laughed. "I like your shoes but you need some practice!"

The shoes looked great, but they made the trip back to campus seem like the longest walk of Bjorn's life. Halfway there a car pulled up beside him. The window rolled down and someone inside offered him $200 to get in the car. Bjorn declined but the corner of his mouth turned up with a hint of a smile. Fucking great costume!

11

The dining hall in Oberholtzer was open only to the few international students who were unable to return home for the Thanksgiving holiday. Even then, it would be closed after 2 pm on Thursday. The students were expected to make their own dinner arrangements. The Americans had mostly cleared out and the dorms were quiet.

Anja sat by herself with a salad and a tranche of turkey covered with mud-colored gravy. The rest of the cafeteria was empty. Bjorn stood paralyzed, tray in hand, realizing he had fallen into a trap. He could approach her or not, but he could not hide among the crowd.

Then she saw him looking and they locked eyes. Like a deer that notices the hunter's rifle a second too late, Bjorn no escape. With a deep breath he walked over to her table.

"Do you mind if I sit here?"

Anja swiveled her head to look around at all the empty seats.

"It's so hard to find a place to sit today," he said, hoping he was funny but fearing he wasn't.

She gestured at the seat across from her. "What part of Canada are you from?" she asked.

"Am I so obvious?"

She laughed. "Did you think you blend in around here?"

Relieved, he set down his tray with turkey, mashed potatoes, sweet potatoes, green beans, corn, gravy, rolls, ham, bowl of salad, Jell-o, pie, coffee, and cup of soda. "I'm from Toronto," he said.

"Me too!" she exclaimed.

They exchanged names and talked about their neighborhoods back home. They knew all the same spots.

"*Gizhide!*" said Bjorn.

Anja laughed. "You speak Ojibwe?"

"I can order off the menu at this Chippewa restaurant I like. Besides food, I know only the one word that perfectly describes this place. It must be destiny."

"You Vikings and your destiny!"

"Norseman," he corrected. "Not all Norsemen are Vikings."

"But you're a true Viking," she said. A thrill ran through him. He knew she was seeing him with more than just her eyes.

"I haven't committed to joining the family business," he said. He covered his face with his hand. He had just admitted to being part of a crime family.

"I'm not a fortune teller," Anja said. "I'm not predicting you're going to join your family. But you seem like a Viking to me. I can't imagine you any other way. Maybe you should be Bjorn the Red for the blood of your enemies stacked up like cordwood around you."

They laughed together. Bjorn grinned. He hoped it was not too frightening a look. Anja's smile was not like his. Her face was made for a smile. She had round cheeks that accentuated the upturned corners of her mouth. Her eyes made crow's feet when she laughed. He knew when she grew old these would become permanent, making her seem perpetually in good cheer. Her hair was long and straight and her figure full and curvy. She was an easy person to be around, even for him.

"You said Houston is *gizhide*," said Anja. "You don't like it in this city? You don't seem comfortable here."

"I love it," said Bjorn. "I'm not comfortable. Everything is difficult and strange. In Toronto my path was well trod and safe. My family is influential and wealthy. Nothing required effort. Here, every day holds a challenge for me. Unexpected things happen all the time. It makes me feel alive. Perhaps I am an exploring Viking instead of a warring Viking."

"Perhaps you are both," she said. "But Bjorn the Red you are. May the gods comfort the widows of your enemies. And your friends."

Taken aback, Bjorn's attention went to her face. Her eyes looked slightly glassy and trancelike. A second later she snapped out of it. A cheery smile returned to her face and a laugh bubbled from her lips.

A shiver of dread traveled down Bjorn's spine.

Bjorn jammed the feeling deep down in his soul for another day. Sorrow might come, but in this moment he would revel in the joy of having Anja's eyes upon him and her words in his ears.

12

"Come back to me," said Bjorn's mother.

"I swore to return when I could fly like grandfather," said Bjorn.

Sveta spun around, startled. She had been staring out of a floor-to-ceiling window overlooking a bleak landscape of gray skies and skeletal trees powdered with snow. However, the room they were in was snug and opulent, outfitted with the trappings of a castle. "Oh! It's you! I hadn't expected you to return to me here, right this second." Her hair was longer and blonder than he remembered, and it was gathered up and braided so that it hung like twin ropes down her back.

"You asked," he said.

"Yes, I did. And this is great, but not the place I want to see you."

"You should have been more specific."

"Really?" she asked. "You're going to be a picky little shit to your mother even in her dreams?"

Bjorn looked around. "Is that where we are?"

"Of course it is! You're down in that fucking American sauna bath called Houston and you left me here by myself!"

"I have five brothers and two sisters all living in Toronto and Dad dotes on you. You're hardly all alone."

"You were the last child who relied on me and made me feel needed. Now I just have the cat and he doesn't even need me."

"He is a cat, mom. He needs no one. And I have not relied on you in years."

"There you are being a shit again."

"I thought you would be proud of my self-reliance. And it hurts my feelings you call me that."

"I've been telling you for years and it never bothered you before."

Bjorn nodded. "I never took it seriously. This time it feels like you mean it."

"I always meant it, but it doesn't mean I don't love you. It's complicated for parents. Maybe it feels real to you because of where we are. Dreams are about emotions so it makes sense you would feel my emotions in my dreams."

Bjorn laughed. "This is MY dream!"

Sveta put her fists on her hips. "I dream about this place every night. I constructed it out of my imagination."

"People don't do that," said Bjorn. "They just dream and their subconscious makes everything up."

"It's called lucid dreaming," said Sveta. "Once you learn it, you are in complete control of your dreams. I can make or do anything I want when I dream."

"Maybe I am the one doing the lucid dreaming."

"You didn't know you were in a dream until I told you."

Bjorn walked over to the fireplace and held his hands before the flames. "This feels like a real fire," he said. "How did you learn to do this?"

"I read a book about it. It's not so hard."

"Really? It seems like magic."

Sveta laughed. "It's not. Anyone can learn it. You just need something to give you a clue that you're dreaming. I use my watch." She tapped the digital watch strapped to her right wrist. "The subconscious is not good with numbers, so if you check your watch and it says something like twenty-seven o'clock or 1:87 pm, you know you're dreaming. Once you realize that, you are lucid dreaming."

"I'm going to have to try that," said Bjorn.

"You, my son, can't learn lucid dreaming because you are a hallucination of my subconscious."

Bjorn shrugged. "Maybe we are both dreaming and I crossed over into yours because I heard you call for me."

Sveta grinned at her boy. "You would be the wizard from a saga!" she said.

"Maybe the hero."

"No, the wizard. The wizard has great power. If the hero is all-powerful then he isn't heroic at all."

"I promise you being the wizard does not make you all powerful."

"Bjorn, you are not a wizard who can travel in dreams. If you were, I would not be able to make you do this!"

Sveta gestured with her hands.

"What?" asked Bjorn. "What is that?"

"I am making you dance."

"Oh!" he exclaimed. "I missed my cue!" Bjorn capered around like a drunken monkey.

"That is not the dance I was trying to make you do, my little shit," she said when he had finished.

Bjorn leaned down and kissed his mother on the forehead. "I'm sorry I got the dance wrong. I will return when I have learned to fly like grandpa," he said.

And then he woke up.

13

Bjorn struggled in Russian class because he found it increasingly difficult to pay attention. A newcomer sat on the other side of Irina. No one else could see them. The visitor was shrouded in black robes and a black hood. Long, billowy sleeves covered their hands. Bjorn could get no glimpse of the foreboding figure's face no matter how hard he tried to look.

"Mr. Unfriend," said Professor Linsky, "What are you looking at?"

"I'm not sure," said Bjorn.

"Can you try to describe it in Russian?"

But Bjorn couldn't describe it with any words at all.

When the class was over, the dark figure did not stand when Irina stood. Bjorn also remained seated. "I'll catch up," he said. When Bjorn was alone with the thing, he heard a voice like the dry rattle of bones.

"Few seek to look upon me."

"It wasn't something I planned on doing," he said, "and I'm regretting it a little right now." Bjorn's throat was dry. This was not like the Manitou who guided Anja. He could feel the power of the spirit. He was speaking to something older, something fundamental to the universe. This was a Major Arcana.

The figure turned its head toward him and he steeled himself to meet the merciless gaze of a skull, but that is not what he saw. Below the black cowl was the wrinkled face of an old woman framed in gray hair. Had she been wearing a pantsuit and walking in the mall he would never have looked twice at her.

"I thought you were Death," he said, gesturing at her heavy robes.

"What is Death?" she asked.

"I just wrote an essay on it for Philosophy. Do you want me to get it out of my backpack for you?"

"Sarcasm in my presence?" she asked. The old woman cracked a smile and narrowed her eyes in a sly look. "You are such a shit to me," she said.

Bjorn felt a cold chill hearing his mother's words. He did not try to make another joke. "Who are you?"

The old woman waved one hand expansively. "Oh, I have so, so many names! But one you will recognize is the Crone. Some do call me Death because I come to those in my domain as their time approaches."

"To take them?"

"To comfort them if I can. Pain leads to death. I would ease their journey or give them the relief they need to find other paths."

"Then why did you ask me about death?" he asked.

"Not for you to explain it to me," she said, "but for you to question your idea of it."

"You sound like my philosophy professor."

"I would make an excellent instructor of philosophy," she said, "because I know the right questions to ask."

"What is the right question to ask me?"

"Why did you joke about a philosophy paper when you sat in the presence of a being worshiped as a god?"

"You already know the answer, don't you?"

"I know the answer."

"Because you know my thoughts."

"Because I know people."

Bjorn swallowed and tried to think. "I wanted to seem brave," he said, "but that's a childish thing, like a mouse standing up to a mountain."

"Your metaphors are shitty," said the Crone.

"I don't think my path is to become a Viking English teacher."

"All for the best," said the Crone. "Bjorn, you could have bowed to me and promised to serve me and sought my favor. But instead of bending to my will, you cracked jokes. A shitty joke, I might add."

"Did I offend you?" Bjorn felt a moment of nervousness. He did not know what the Crone could do to him if her angered her.

"Offend?" she scoffed. "Who am I to be offended by a kitten? Joking in the presence of power requires bravery. Cowardice would have disappointed me."

"Why?"

"What good is it to your people if the one gifted to see the true world doesn't have the will to exert himself? Cowardice robs humanity of its greatest champions." The Crone stood. "Time is short and you have not asked the question in your heart."

"I didn't know I got to ask a question," said Bjorn.

"You already asked me several questions."

"That was just conversation."

The Crone shrugged and prompted him with an arched eyebrow.

He cleared his throat. "The doom that comes for Irina— can I avert it?"

"You would pay a price to do so."

"What do you want? Would I have to trade years of my life for hers or something like that?"

"I'm not some petty demon bargaining for your soul. The cost you pay will be the things you must give up to create this change. Every thing you choose means a thing you reject. It is a cost you charge yourself. I want nothing from you."

"But I don't know the cost," said Bjorn.

"That is the way of mortals."

"This game is rigged," said Bjorn.

"That is the way of mortals."

Bjorn nodded. "Fine. I'll do what I must to change Irina's doom. Will you help me?"

"I will," said the Crone. "Look for me at the darkest point. It will be your only opportunity. But for this assistance you must do something for me in return when I call upon you. You are bound to this beyond time and life and desire."

"Wait!" said Bjorn. "You just said you wanted nothing from me!"

But the Crone was gone.

14

"It is so hard to trust immortal spirits," said Bjorn around a mouthful of meat loaf and gravy, "Because everything they say comes from a place of knowing more than we do. We don't always know what our actions or words really mean, but they do. It is an unfair advantage."

Anja arched one eyebrow, which reminded Bjorn of the Crone. "You sound like you speak to spirits on a regular basis."

Bjorn shrugged. The Manitou stood nearby, his muscular arms crossed in front of his chest in annoyance. "Everyone speaks to spirits. That is what prayer is."

"Prayer isn't a conversation. It's a note that goes into a suggestion box."

"What about you?" he asked. "What is your connection to the spirit world?"

Bjorn waited while Anja chewed a spoonful of peas that had been boiled until flavorless. "Maybe," she said, "I don't have a connection to the spirit world. Maybe you are just assuming that because I'm Chippewa I'm some sort of woodland mystic. Maybe you are stereotyping."

"Maybe I *am* stereotyping a little bit."

"Maybe you are stereotyping a fuckton. Instead of chanting in the woods, maybe I'm going to be a scientist studying chemicals and discovering new substances that change the world."

Bjorn shrugged. "Sure, why not?"

"I'm going to be a scientist."

"Maybe you can study chemicals and discover the spirits hiding inside them."

"You are an asshole," she said, but she was laughing. "I can't always tell when you're joking or just an idiot."

"I could be both. You could be both too. Scientist and mystic, I mean, not idiot and joker. I am the idiot and joker. But whichever you pick, I'm thankful I sat down at your table." Anja blushed and suddenly directed her attention at cutting a bite off her roast beef.

"Because we met on Thanksgiving…" said Bjorn.

The Manitou rolled his huge eyes.

"Smooth."

15

"I'm surprised you came," said Kev from the other cot a few feet away.

"I'm surprised you asked me," said Bjorn.

"We're roommates. We're friends," said Kev nonchalantly.

Bjorn would have described them as friends of circumstance, people who were friendly because of proximity. He liked Kev okay, but doubted either of them would drive across town to visit the other, especially since Bjorn seemed to find so many ways to irritate Kev. Despite that, Kev was one of Bjorn's closest friends here. It was a sad realization.

"Why are you surprised I would come?" asked Bjorn.

"I don't know. You're so… intense all the time. Coming to a blood drive is a nice thing to do, but also low key. We sit in lounge chairs with needles in our arms and squeeze a ball for a few minutes and then drink lemonade and eat a cookie. It's walking in a park, not climbing a mountain."

"And that does not seem like me?"

"No, dude, no. Like, if you were donating blood I would expect you to burst through the door with a machete and hack off your hand so the blood could flow into a ritual chalice. There would be organ music in the background."

"If we were planning to drink the blood as part of a ritual, that is precisely what I would do."

"Fuck me," said Kev.

"What is wrong?"

"I think I'm starting to get your sense of humor."

16

Anja studied a lot.

Bjorn sat cross legged on the 1950's-era brown carpet that covered her floor, the back of his head touching the windowsill. She had the same kind of room he had: a two-person room with bunkbeds, two end tables, two desks and two chairs. Opposite the window was the door to the bathroom shared with the other room in the suite.

Bjorn balanced his math book in his lap but wasn't paying much attention to it. He should have taken the next class instead of the one he was in. Bjorn picked math up easily; it was his safe subject. He was thinking about petitioning for a waiver so he could get into a more challenging class without finishing the prerequisite.

Anja was good in math, but good was not always good enough. She sat on the upper bunk, her Organic Chem book open on her lap.

"I'm getting these wrong," she said. She was frustrated and her voice sounded like a cat that had been drenched with a bucket of water. Elise, one of Anja's O Chem classmates, had left earlier after breaking down and crying. Elise had received a D on the last test and had been falling behind ever since.

"Kev told me a lot of Chemical Engineers change majors to Business after they take O Chem."

"Yes, it's the grim reaper of engineering," said Anja.

"The Grim Reaper isn't so bad once you get to know her," said Bjorn.

Anja looked up. "What the fuck, Bjorn?"

"Don't pay attention to me," he said. He had tried to help Anja with the math part of the work, but he didn't understand the chemistry so there was little he could do.

"I feel like I know this, but my answers are all off," she said.

"What grade do you have?"

"I've got a B."

"That's really good for making a lot of math mistakes."

"A few."

"Yeah, that's what I meant," Bjorn said.

"Anja closed her eyes. "If I concentrate, I can visualize the molecule. It helps me a lot."

A glow appeared around Anja's head. Bjorn normally didn't see auras unless he tried, but Anja's was clear and bright. He squinted and leaned forward attentively. The halo grew whiter and brighter until it was as if a powerful lightbulb was directly behind her head.

"I'm picturing the molecule now," she said. "I can see it vividly, including lots of permutations. Carbon molecules can be twisted into different shapes and that changes their properties, so it helps me a lot in class to be able to imagine them like this."

To Bjorn's eyes, Anja's aura glowed like the halo of a saint. Beams of light radiated in all directions connecting her to the universe.

"Holy scientist," whispered Bjorn, "That must be fantastic during a test."

17

Bjorn woke up to the sound of Kev thrashing on the lower bunk. His eyes were gummy and his first thought was "*Ya nyeznayu.*" It took a moment to remember the phrase meant "I don't know."

Bjorn climbed out of the bunk and went to the bathroom where he peed like a full blast garden hose. He finished, washed his hands, and splashed water on his face. He had been up until three o'clock studying with Irina for their Russian test. He came away from the session feeling like the only Russian he understood was *Ya nyeznayu.*

Back in his room, the clock radio said it was 4:18. No wonder he was tired. Bjorn took the chair from his desk and moved it next to Kev's bunk. He sat by his roommate, who was still thrashing and sweating in his sleep.

"Kev Armitage," said Bjorn.

Kev opened his eyes, but they were unfocused and fixed on nothing.

"What is wrong, Kev?"

"I can't get away," whispered Kev. "It doesn't matter where I hide. She always finds me."

"It's a dream. Wake up."

Bjorn shook Kev, but Kev did not respond. He snapped his fingers in front of his roommate's eyes, but they did not blink. He slapped Kev on the cheeks. When that failed, Bjorn got his glass and filled it with water. He was about to pour it on Kev's face when he stopped and placed the cup on his desk.

"This is probably a bad idea," Bjorn said to himself, but he felt excited too. If he did it once, he could do it again.

Bjorn lounged in the chair, put his chin on his chest, crossed his arms, and closed his eyes. He let his exhaustion overtake him. In moments his consciousness faded.

Kevin of the Armitages!

Bjorn found himself in a nighttime forest where the plants looked like twisted corals. "Kevin of the Armitages!" he called again, pushing his way through scaly fan-shaped fronds and skirting around growths like pulsating brains. He plunged into the clicking and screeching of the forest following the sounds of screaming. Prickly bushes tore at his skin as he hiked.

His mother said lucid dreaming let her control her dreams. If she could, so could he. Bjorn paused and concentrated. "I need armor," he said, exerting his will over the dream world around him. His clothes changed into stiff leather with a heavy chainmail shirt, knee-high boots and thick gloves. He held a round shield in his left hand and an axe in his right.

When he burst into the clearing, the first thing Bjorn saw was Kev lying in the prickly grass, naked, arms and legs splayed. Serpents clung to him by their fangs like leeches. Nearby stood a tall and slender woman wearing familiar robes, the same robes he had seen on All Hallows. Her eyeless face was flawless beauty, but when she spoke, her mouth was like a lamprey with rows of needle teeth descending into the back of her throat. "Come to me now, Son of the Crow. I smell you on the air. Put your mouth on my body and I shall put mine on yours!"

"You are not putting that mouth on anything of mine," said Bjorn.

"I want to feel you inside me so I can taste that burning energy I sense in your soul."

"Absolutely fucking not!"

"You must! Do you not long for a woman to draw forth ecstasy from your manhood?"

Bjorn immediately felt the beating of his heart in every vein of his body. Each pulse was more intense than the last. He felt his cock harden until it was a rock, painfully constrained by his clothes. Bjorn bent over and tried to push his penis down. "You are the worst!" he said to the creature.

"Bjorn!" said Kev. "You came for me. Help! Get me out of here!"

"You cannot fight me," hissed the creature.

"This is a dream! I am lucid dreaming so I can do anything!" said Bjorn, hurling his axe. The blade sunk itself deep in the beast's chest. With a swift turn the sexual arousal became fierce anger. Bjorn was buffeted with hate and fear and pain. He felt squeezed and diminished, assaulted by winds of emotion that pulled at the tattered edges of his mind. He was eroding. Tears leaked from his eyes. He had to escape before he was lost.

Bjorn's head popped up. He looked around frantically. The dorm room was quiet except for Kev tossing and turning in his sheets. So much for fighting. He reached over and grabbed the cup of water from the desk. But before he poured it over Kev he stopped and set the water back down. His boxer shorts looked like a tent. He went into the bathroom, took off his clothes, stepped into the shower and turned the water on cold. He stayed under the water until he was washed clean of the creature's filthy arousal.

Bjorn dried off, dressed and went back to Kev's side, then poured the water over his friend's face.

Kev spluttered as if he were drowning, took a deep breath and looked relieved.

"You woke me out of my nightmare," Kev said.

"As soon as I could," said Bjorn. But then he shrugged. "Almost as soon as I could."

18

"...that was the dream," said Bjorn, "and I've been having difficulty all week. I'm easily startled and I keep thinking I see the creature in crowds. I've been… emotional." Bjorn shifted, crinkling the paper that covered the examination table dominating the small room.

"What do you mean by emotional?" asked the doctor.

"I'm not used to lots of emotions."

"Everyone has emotions."

Bjorn nodded. He was staring at his feet. "I know that of course. Sometimes I feel powerful emotions. But mine are orderly. I know what they are doing and why. This week has been chaos. Everything is fine and then suddenly I am angry or afraid or sad or lonely. I told my friend and she said I am having male PMS. Then she laughed. I wept and she finally became concerned and told me to see a doctor. I don't even know what male PMS is."

"There isn't any such thing as male PMS," said the doctor, "but I don't think there's much I can do for you. I'm a general practitioner. It sounds like you need a psychiatrist. We don't have a psychiatrist in the student clinic. You're going to have to go off campus for that."

Bjorn didn't like that idea. He didn't want to tell a psychiatrist he was seeing toothy lamprey mouths gaping in the shadows. Psychiatrists were notorious for their skepticism of visions, voices, auras, precognition, ghosts, and all sorts of other things that made up Bjorn's regular days.

"Maybe you could just give me something for indigestion?" asked Bjorn.

19

"What did the doctor say?" asked Irina. They sat in overstuffed armchairs in the basement of Taub Hall. They had met here to watch the latest *MacGyver* episode on the dorm TV, but neither was following the story. They were just waiting for MacGyver to build something with a paperclip.

"The doctor said I should see a psychiatrist."

"Psychiatrists have never helped me," she said. "I was hoping he could give you a pill or something."

"I don't like taking medicines."

"Of course you don't," she said, patting him on the cheek in a condescending gesture. Her hand lingered a second longer than it had to. "You don't like anything that makes life easier or better or more fun."

"You make me sound bleak," he said.

"It's one of the things I like about you. You don't need anything but you."

"Now you are making me *feel* bleak."

"I'm envious. I wish I didn't need anything but me."

Words died on Bjorn's lips. He could feel the despair and loneliness behind her voice.

"You're not alone—"

"Ah ah!" Irina exclaimed. "I don't tolerate platitudes."

Bjorn felt relieved. It was easy to say words of comfort, but they always felt like little lies to him. "How about we just spend time suffering together then?" he asked.

She closed her eyes and smiled a small but genuine smile. "That is the best way to suffer."

20

Bjorn walked from corner to corner of his room holding a small bundle of smoldering herbs over his head. The wisp of smoke left its distinctive odor everywhere.

"What the hell are you doing?" Kev asked as soon as he walked through the door.

"I'm burning sage. It cleanses a place of evil spirits."

"It will also cleanse a place of roommates and anyone with a nose."

"It does not smell so bad. You will get used to it."

"I don't want to get used to it! I want you to stop!"

Bjorn turned to his roommate. "You are plagued by nightmares every night. You can't sleep. You look like you're falling apart. I am trying to help you."

Kev's annoyance waned at that. "Thanks, I appreciate it. I really do. But Voodoo isn't going to solve my sleeping problems. I went to the doctor and he gave me a prescription for a sleep aid so I can finally get some rest."

"Then you will not be able to wake up. I don't think that is a good idea."

"Pouring water on my face to wake me up can't go on any

longer," said Kev. "I can't get my mattress dry and it's starting to smell like mildew."

"Your problem is that you're still sleeping with Mary from that paranormal club."

"Also Sharon sometimes. But not at the same time," he said. "Yet."

"You are turning into a dog," said Bjorn.

"Woman's best friend. But Mary and Sharon have nothing to do with my problem."

Kev had bags under his eyes and his cheeks were hollowing out. He looked like he forgot to comb his hair and he was thoroughly rumpled.

"That club is the problem. You have to get out of it."

"It is the bright spot in my existence. No way am I quitting that club. My parents have plans for me. My grandparents have plans for me. Even my friends have plans. I'm not doing super great on anything I'm supposed to do to make everyone else happy, but the one goal I set for myself I'm accomplishing like a boss."

"Kev…"

"Nope! Not going to discuss it. In fact, I'm going there right now."

"Why now?"

"Nooners," Kev said, and left the room.

Kev was going to be difficult. It was hard to save someone from a burning building if they kept running back in every time you took them out. The room was clear of dark influences, but sage was a simple tool, not a miracle. It couldn't keep out the creature from Kev's dreams, especially if Kev kept returning to the house where it resided. Bjorn had a plan, but it was experimental.

He closed his eyes and reached out with his mind.

"Manitou," he said, but nothing happened.

"Manitou!" he said again, calling more forcefully. Still nothing happened.

"Manitou!" he said a third time, not just calling but exerting his will, trying to bend the world to his wishes.

"You are so loud!" said the Manitou.

"I thought you might ignore me."

"I did ignore you, but you shouted louder each time. Can't you take a hint?"

Bjorn shrugged.

"Why are you bothering me?"

"I need help," said Bjorn.

"I am a Manitou of the People. Why don't you ask one of your Norse gods for help?"

"You know what they are like. Would you ask them for help if you had a choice?"

"I have no reason to help you, Bjorn."

"There is one reason, O Manitou! You are far from your lands and no one seeks you here, not even Anja. But I do. I value your wisdom and strength."

The Manitou sneered but did not leave. "What?"

"I wish to consecrate this room to the Manitou of the People."

"What the fuck?" said the Manitou.

"There is a dark spirit that frequents this room. I wish to consecrate it to bar them from entry."

"That's not how sacred places work for the People. Places are sacred either because spirits live there or because the memory of the People resides there, like at a burial site. You can't shake around some sage and make this room sacred. Using sage to clear a place isn't even from our part of the land."

"No, it isn't, but sage or no sage is a detail, like the difference between Christians baptizing babies or baptizing adults."

The Manitou snorted. "Go ask a Catholic or a Baptist if those are small differences!"

"The People differ from each other in particulars but they

71

share basic beliefs. Are you not a Manitou of the Earth no matter what tribe walks upon it? You are revered by the Chippewa, but also by the Saginaw, Pawnee, Arapaho, and many others. The sage is irrelevant."

"This still isn't how it's done."

"That's why I called you. You are with Anja here in the Quad, so a spirit does live here. You can make this land sacred."

"I live in Law Hall, not Sett," said the Manitou. "This plan will not work."

"Is there anything you can do for me?" asked Bjorn.

The Manitou stepped forward. "Since you asked, there is one thing I can do." He took the thumb of his right hand and pressed it on Bjorn's forehead between his eyes. Bjorn felt a burning that spread like a wave across his entire head.

"That hurts. How do I make the headache go away?" asked Bjorn.

"Willow bark."

"Where do I get willow bark around here?"

"Take two aspirin."

Bjorn rolled his eyes. "What did you do to me?"

"I called your spirit animal guide," said the Manitou.

"I thought you had to be of the People to have a spirit animal?"

"No. Everyone has a spirit animal, but few who are not of the People build a relationship with them. Yours just doesn't like you."

"Why would it not like me? I've never even met it."

"It knows you."

Just then a black bird settled on the outside ledge of the window. It shuffled from foot to foot, preened its feathers, and cocked an eye in the room. The Manitou gestured toward the bird.

"That?" asked Bjorn, his voice deflated. "It's a little bird. I thought it might be a bear or a wolf. A cougar would have been good too! That's the school mascot. I've watched the handlers walk Shasta around campus a few times in the evenings. I would love to talk to her!"

"That attitude," said the Manitou, "is why the crow does not like you." Then the Manitou was gone.

"You left before I could say thank you," said Bjorn to the air, but he was not sure he would have thanked the Manitou at all.

21

"What do you know about crows?" asked Bjorn.

"Crows?" asked Anja around a bite of toast with jam. She and Bjorn had fallen into the habit of having lunch together in the cafeteria on Mondays, Wednesdays, and Fridays, but their schedules did not align for lunch on Tuesdays and Thursdays. On those days they came in early and had a long breakfast with several mugs of terrible coffee. They talked about Toronto, how they missed cold weather, their favorite foods they could not find in the South, grades, and the crazy things Americans said.

This was the first time crows had come into the conversation.

"Well…" she said, "I'm not an expert, but they're in the Corvus family along with ravens. Crows are really smart and they hold grudges."

"Grudges? But they are animals."

"Yeah, but if you cross a crow it will remember your face."

"Oh great!"

Anja laughed. "Did you piss off a crow?"

"I guess so. I'm not sure what I did."

"Maybe it will fly away and leave you alone."

Bjorn pointed toward the cafeteria windows where a crow perched on a windowsill.

"No way!" said Anja. "It followed you? It's like that Alfred Hitchcock movie."

"It follows me all over," he said as he layered a slab of ham on bread followed by two circles of pineapple, lettuce, Swiss cheese, and another piece of bread slathered with mayonnaise.

"How have you tried to get rid of it?"

"I haven't," Bjorn said. "I want to make friends with it."

"You make friends with something?" asked Anja.

"I have friends," he said.

She laughed. "Okay, if you say so. I would suggest feeding it, but your choice of food might make it angrier."

"What?"

"Pineapple on a sandwich?"

"It goes well with ham."

"You eat everything! It must be really gross in there," she said, leaning across the table and poking him in the belly with one finger. A surprised look crossed her face and she poked him again. "You're not as spongy as I thought." She leaned a little farther and used her whole hand to feel his stomach. "Damn, Bjorn, you have some muscles."

Then her complexion deepened into a blush and she sat back and averted her eyes. "Sorry about that."

Bjorn's eyes were wide and his head felt like he had just downed a glass of hard liquor. He had planned to ask Anja more about crows, see if she believed in Manitou, and lots of other things, but all he could think of was that she liked his muscles.

22

No more than eight students and the instructor gathered in the classroom. The chairs and tables had been pushed aside and four bodies lay strewn on the shiny white tile floor.

"I didn't think you'd come to this either," said Kev.

"Why not?" asked Bjorn. "This is not as low-key as giving blood." One of his hands was clasped behind the other, fingers interwoven, his arms straight, palm on the chest of the body before him. He thrust down with a steady rhythm, compressing the plastic training dummy.

"Learning how to save someone's life is life-affirming, you know?" said Kev.

"Yes. And?"

"And you're more like a wolf. I can't imagine a wolf doing CPR."

"Wolves don't have hands."

"But if they did."

"What about you?" asked Bjorn. "You're a cynic prowling for sex. I don't see why you're here unless you're interested in the female practice dummy."

"She would look hot in the right outfit," said Kev.

"Seriously."

"Okay, seriously. You're right; I am a cynic. I don't believe in anyone or anything so if someone has to be saved I need to do it myself."

"They'll die eventually anyway, so why bother?" asked Bjorn.

"I'm a cynic, not a nihilist. Of course they'll die eventually, but they have to do that on their own time, not mine."

Bjorn paused his compressions and looked his roommate in the eyes. "That is worthy of a Viking."

"Switch!" said the instructor, who was standing in front of them now. "If you do the compressions correctly you are likely to crack the ribs, but it is better to save someone's life with cracked ribs than let them die intact. Bjorn, you would have caused massive internal injuries with your compressions. You need to go a bit lighter."

"See, you're a wolf!" said Kev as he knelt by the dummy and began compressions. "Or maybe a bear."

"Exactly what I was thinking! Can you believe someone said I am like a crow?"

"I don't see that at all."

"I know, right?"

23

"I thought we were going to study for the final," said Irina. The Crone stood behind Irina, features hidden by the dark robes.

"I wasn't able to make it," said Bjorn. He did not acknowledge the Crone.

"What's wrong?" Irina asked.

"Why do you think something's wrong?"

"You're smiling."

Bjorn was smiling indeed. As the Crone had said, every choice excluded something else. Bjorn had sacrificed his time to study for the Russian final so he could help Anja study for her O Chem final. He sat very close to her on her bed the night before, their feet dangling off the bunk. She smelled of leather and the argan oil that made her hair glossy. Below that was the flowery soap smell that clung to her skin and her own natural scent. They were so close!

"Can we go through that again?" he remembered Anja asking as she brushed a strand of hair out of her eyes. Anja put her hand down and it landed on Bjorn's. Both of them froze, then turned their heads to each other. Their lips were inches apart. A magnetic force seemed to pull him toward her.

The door banged open and Anja's tall and perpetually angry roommate charged through. "Do you have any extra Blue Books? I dropped mine in a puddle and ruined it and I won't be able to go to the bookstore before the Sociology final tomorrow morning."

"Top drawer of my desk," said Anja with a wave of her hand. When she put it down it was once again over Bjorn's.

The roommate saw where the hand landed. She looked from one to the other, suspicion crossing her face. "I guess the two of you have been studying really hard."

"Uh huh. For hours," said Anja.

"Do you two need me to go away for a while?" the roommate asked. "If I have to, I can crash at my boyfriend's for the night."

Bjorn looked to Anja. He had not thought that might be a possibility. He held his breath as he waited for her answer.

"No," she said. "We're just studying."

Bjorn let out his breath slowly so it would not be obvious he had been holding it. He could not help feeling disappointed, but Anja's soft fingers on the back of his hand counseled him to be patient.

So, yes, he had skipped his study session. He wanted good grades, but last night had been worth tanking his Russian final.

"You're probably going to fail," said Irina.

"You might be right."

"It didn't have to be that way," she said. She sounded irritated. "I'm trying to help you. You should stop pushing away the people who try to look out for you."

Bjorn found himself inside the dark place in Irina's soul where she was cold and alone, yet hard and strong. He could feel her annoyance with him. Part of her was trying to do something good for him, to prove that she could make a difference to someone else. She wanted to know that she mattered. Irina felt bitter and disappointed that she had failed her only friend.

Her only friend?

Bjorn's stomach churned. The Russian final was not just the Russian final; studying was not just studying. He felt as if he had betrayed Irina through carelessness and selfishness. All his joy turned to ashes in a moment. What could he do or say at this point to salvage this mess?

"You have already helped me so much this semester," he said. "All the times we have studied have made a big difference. Whatever grade I get will be because of you."

Irina frowned at him. Too late did he realize that if he failed, it would be a condemnation of her help. Irina turned and strode into class for the final. Bjorn shuffled along after. Professor Linsky made everyone sit in staggered rows, then passed each student a stapled packet.

Bjorn looked over the first page of questions. It started with conjugating verbs. He could do that, but the second page was question and response. He stared at the Cyrillic letters, trying to force them to whisper their meaning to him.

The Crone came up beside him. "The Crow is known for wisdom," she said, "but not because he is smarter than everyone else. He is wise because he fucked up and learned to do better."

"I should have thought about Irina," Bjorn whispered so only the Crone could hear him.

"Idiot!" she replied. "The wise man knows that a decision may carry good and bad whichever path he chooses. What separates him from the fool is that he chooses which evil he is willing to live with."

Bjorn rolled his eyes. He expected more out of the Crone than a parental lecture.

"But I promised you help," she said. The Crone placed her hand on his shoulder and the Cyrillic words in front of him suddenly became simple and obvious. The test was basic conversations a child could answer. Then she removed her hand and walked away. The clarity immediately began to fade.

"Hey! Crone!" he whispered, "come back!"

The Crone did not return. The Cyrillic letters were again a struggle for him, but now they seemed more familiar, like a word on the tip of his tongue. If he mouthed the words while reading along, answers came to him like dialogue from old movies he had seen many times.

"Time is up," said Professor Linsky much later.

"I'm on the last question," said Bjorn.

"Time is up, Mr. Unfriend. You have to put your pen down."

Bjorn scrawled the last few words as fast as he could, put his pen down, and flipped the page to the back of the packet. He stood and walked to the front of the room where he put his test on the top of the stack. He and Professor Linsky were alone in the room.

"Where is everyone?" Bjorn asked.

"You are the last to finish, Mr. Unfriend. How do you think you did?"

"*Horosho*," said Bjorn with a grin.

Professor Linsky's brows went up. "I hope you did," said the professor returning a smile. "And the semester's over so I won't correct your pronunciation. I know you've been struggling in this class, but I can tell you're doing your best. I hope you stick with it. Have a good Christmas break and I'll see you in January."

"I will try not to let you down," said Bjorn, thinking of the skipped study session. He hoped he wouldn't always have to pay for pleasure with guilt.

24

The knock on the door was more of a pounding. Bjorn put his book down, annoyed at the interruption, and opened the door.

A short, curvy girl stood at the door wearing a red NASA t-shirt so large he could not tell if she wore shorts or a skirt beneath it. It was Becky, the RA. She held a clipboard in her left hand.

"You know the rules, Unfrid."

"I do. And thank you for pronouncing my name correctly."

"Then why are you making me write you up? It's finals week. All you had to do was get through a couple more days without screwing up. Now I have to do paperwork instead of studying for my ELEE test."

"Then don't write me up. Why would you want to anyway?"

The RA barged past him into the room. "It's serious if I catch you using drugs," she said. "I can't ignore that."

"You could."

"Can't."

"But I'm not doing drugs anyway."

"I could smell your smoke all the way down the hallway." She looked around the small room and then stalked over to his desk where she grabbed the thick roll of sage from the saucer where Bjorn had placed it. She held it in front of her face looking shocked. "Wow. You are really doing this wrong."

"That's not marijuana."

"That's just one of the ways you're doing it wrong. What is this?"

"It's sage. It's for cleansing evil spirits from a place."

"That is the most passive-aggressive thing I have heard anyone say all semester. How do you think this makes Kev feel?"

"I'm not trying to get rid of Kev. And it's not marijuana."

"You're not supposed to be burning random weeds in your room either," said the RA.

"You could give me a warning," he said.

"Freshmen haven't earned leniency yet," she said. "I'm writing you up for… starting a fire in your room. You mess up again before finals are over and you'll be kicked out of the dorm."

The clipboard held the write-up form. She filled it out while he stood waiting. When she finished, she handed him one of the carbon copies and then stalked out of the room. "You mess with Becky and I'll be your worst nightmare!" she said.

"Assistant worst nightmare, at best," he said to the empty room.

25

The December sun was low and bright but the air was cold. It was not cold like Toronto, but as cold as Houston was likely to get. The air was laden with moisture, the kind of cold that oozed through sweaters and cloth and chilled to the bone. Staying warm and comfortable would require leather or thick fabrics to keep out the watery air. But Bjorn did not wear a jacket, just a long-sleeved flannel. He wanted to feel the cold. It was like an old friend he had not encountered in a long time.

He tossed his last French fry onto the sidewalk where the crow that followed him everywhere pounced on it. Bjorn was sitting on a bench in front of the A.D. Bruce Religion building. It was a short walk from Settegast, which was still in sight. The glass religion center building nestled in park-like grounds sprinkled with trees. It was one of the most beautiful places on campus.

"Are we friends yet?" asked Bjorn.

The bird did not answer, but Bjorn figured it must feel differently about him since it was getting fat from all the fries he fed it.

"I have a favor to ask," said Bjorn. The bird ruffled its feathers and flew off. Bjorn sighed. "As I expected."

The days were short, and night would be coming soon. He hurried back to his room. He knew Kev would be there. His roommate was caught between overwhelming finals and torturous nightmares. He took sleeping pills that trapped him in his dreams, but when he woke he was more exhausted than when he went to sleep.

Kev was going home for Christmas break. This was the last night Bjorn could attempt to help him. Bjorn had only recently shaken off the effects of the first time he faced the spirit in Kev's dreams, and he did not feel any more prepared now than he had been then. But if he did nothing, Kev would be trapped with that spirit for the entire month of Christmas break.

When Bjorn walked in, he heard Kev sniffling. Kev sat on his bed, elbows on knees, back hunched, looking defeated.

"Is something wrong?"

Kev shook his head no. "I think I'm coming down with a little cold," he said. Kev's eyes were watery and Bjorn spotted the tracks of tears. He did not buy that Kev was getting sick.

"Are you sad?"

"No."

"Have you taken your sleeping pill yet?"

"I don't want to. I don't want to go to sleep anymore."

"You have to sleep sometime."

"I feel like I'm in a Nightmare on Elm Street movie," said Kev.

Bjorn brought his chair next to his roommate's bed. "Lie down," he said.

"What are you doing?"

When Kev had lain down, Bjorn put his hand on Kev's forehead. "Sleep!" he said.

A minute crept by, then another.

"Are you trying to put me to sleep psychically?" asked Kev, "Or is it more of a power of suggestion thing?"

"Just an experiment," said Bjorn.

"I need to know because your intent determines how I'm going to ridicule you."

"And what would the intent be behind your ridicule?" asked Bjorn. "Because your intent determines how long I will bludgeon you with my fists."

"We could play cards?" offered Kev.

"Much better idea."

They broke out a deck of cards and played Hearts long into the night. Bjorn became so tired he could not fathom how Kev was still awake.

"Your go," said Bjorn, but his roommate did not take his turn. Bjorn looked up from his cards and saw that Kev's head had slumped over and drool ran down from the corner of his mouth onto his shoulder.

Bjorn gathered up the cards and set them on his desk. "Let's try this," he said, leaning over Kev to once again trace the rune for Thor above his roommate's forehead. Then he settled back into his chair and closed his eyes. He felt himself drifting to sleep almost immediately.

Bjorn stood on a narrow rocky strand between unclimbable cliffs and choppy grey waves that reflected the brooding sky. Above the cliffs, tiny birds wheeled and turned. Foam splashed across his feet, flung by the waves that crashed on the stony shore. He wore his chainmail and a smooth steel cap with a nose guard. His shield was strapped to his left arm. He hitched his axe into his belt so he could use his hand to climb over the boulders.

The waves were so loud he could barely hear the distant screaming.

"I'm coming!" Bjorn yelled. It was slow going.

A crow landed just out of arm's reach.

"I did not expect to see you here."

"Unfriend," the crow said.

"Really? You too?"

Then the crow launched itself at him, striking him in the throat, its beating wings flashing feathers in his face. He tried to push the bird away with his free hand. Then he felt a snapping at his neck and the crow made off with a chain attached to an amulet.

"I didn't realize I was wearing that," Bjorn said, but he was nevertheless furious that the bird would steal it from him. "This is my dream and I am in control here!" His mother had told him as much, so he expected it to be true. He reached out and willed the bird to return. The crow cawed and it sounded like laughter.

"Well then, if I can't make you come back, I'll fly with you. My dream, my rules," he said. "I hope!" Bjorn willed himself to fly and immediately left the ground. His arms lengthened and flattened, turned black with feathers. He shrank and changed until he matched the bird ahead. He felt the air in a new way. Stretching his arms in long, powerful beats, he began to gain on the mischievous bird, who led him up, up until they were staring into the grey sky above and the birds that flew over the cliffs.

Soon Bjorn realized the tiny birds above the cliffs were not birds at all but huge pterodactyls diminished by distance.

The crow leveled out and ducked into a cave in the cliff face. Bjorn followed. The bird alighted on a stone and dropped the talisman. Bjorn could see the talisman for the first time now, a small disk engraved with the rune *Kaunaz*, representing knowledge. "Of course that's what it was," said Bjorn. "Following knowledge brought me here. But where is here? He retrieved the talisman and put it in his pocket.

The cave was full of a shifting, ruddy light thrown by a brazier of leaping flames. A war chariot was parked in the center of the cave. It had fallen apart with age, wooden pieces rotting and metal rusting. Still in the tresses was a team of enormous horned goats decomposed to skeletons.

"Tanngrisnir and Tanngnjóstr," said Bjorn, touching each goat's skull. "This is unpleasantly dystopian."

At the back of the cave stood a stone altar, but before the altar lay the skeleton of the largest man Bjorn had ever seen. Upon the altar lay a short-handled war hammer. "I imagine this skeleton is supposed to be Thor," he said. "The lamprey spirit probably moved this here after I inscribed Thor's rune on Kev's forehead. The rune can't do Kev any good if its power is hidden and inaccessible."

The crow merely cawed in reply.

Bjorn stepped over the skeleton. He discarded his shield so he could grasp the hammer with both hands. When he touched it, his body vibrated with energy. Even a dream of the hammer possessed power. He turned and walked to the cave entrance, where he threw himself off the cliff. As he fell, he willed himself to turn again into a bird. He dove and turned, flying along the rocky shore. When he could hear the screaming once more, he flapped his wings, picking up speed.

Soon, he found Kev. He was chained to a rock, his lower body in a tidal pool. The red water frothed with carnivorous fish devouring his roommate's flesh.

Bjorn alighted and resumed his normal form. The hammer was still in his hand.

"Bjorn," said Kev, weeping. "I'm dying!"

"No, you're not."

Bjorn strode forward and swung the hammer with all his strength, and the chain binding Kev shattered into a million pieces. The boulder behind the chain cracked. Bjorn pulled Kev out of the water.

"I'm in agony!" groaned Kev.

"No, you're not."

Kev stopped weeping.

"Oh, you're right. Now that you say it, I don't feel

anything at all." The agony and terror drained from Kev's face to be replaced by confusion.

"Let me help you up." Bjorn pulled him to his feet.

"How am I standing? I'm just a skeleton from the waist down."

"It's a dream."

"More like a cartoon. I'm a really crappy cartoon character." Kev did a little jig. "How can I move like that without muscles?"

"You did not have much muscle in the first place."

Kev shot him a look.

"You cannot hurt me with that villager's charm, Son of the Crow," said a voice from behind Bjorn. He turned to see the eyeless spirit. This time she glittered from neck to ankle, sheathed in a serpentine dress made of silver scales that rippled with each step she took. "You have no dominion here."

"I know," said Bjorn.

The spirit gestured and the shattered chains came together and reformed. "This time I will make enough shackles for you both."

"I'm not planning to stay," said Bjorn. "I just came to deliver this to the one who does have dominion here."

Bjorn placed the hammer in Kev's hands.

"Me?" You have got to be joking!"

"The best we can hope for in life is a chance to fight back. This is your dream," said Bjorn. "Take control of it."

And then Bjorn woke up. He watched over his roommate into the early morning. Kev slept restlessly but did not thrash about or whimper in suffering. Eventually Bjorn fell asleep in the chair. When he woke, Bjorn was alone but a blanket had been draped over him and pulled up to his chin.

Kev's bags were gone. He had an early flight and wouldn't have had the time to get much rest. But perhaps he would sleep on the plane.

26

Bjorn felt alone. Kev was gone, Irina was gone, Anja was gone, and so also the Manitou and the Crone. Only those international students unable to return to their native countries were allowed in the dorms over Christmas break. It was a tiny group of strangers. Becky was the Christmas break RA.

"Checkers?" Becky asked. She leaned against Bjorn's doorframe, her arms crossed under her boobs, all her weight on one leg, which accentuated her hip. Her huge, green t-shirt hung on her like a sheet draped across a racing car. It was 1:29 a.m.

"You want to play checkers at one thirty in the morning?"

"Aren't you bored?"

"I'm reading *Njal's Saga*," he said.

"You're worse off than I thought."

"It is an excellent book," he said, but he stepped aside to let her in. "But I guess I can take a break to play."

"Great!" she said. "I need to go back to my room to get the checkerboard. I'll be right back." She raced barefoot to her room at the end of the hall. A moment later she returned with the board and a small box of checkers in one hand and bags of chips, pretzels, and Funyons in the other.

"You have drinks?" she asked.

Kev had a small dorm fridge next to his desk. There were two brown bottles of root beer left on the empty shelves. Bjorn could replace them later.

Becky sat cross-legged and had the board set up in the middle of the floor by the time Bjorn removed the bottle tops and placed a root beer in front of her. "Why checkers?" he asked. "I thought that was a kid's game."

She shot him a look. "You think so? I'll crush you, Mr. Viking. I'm the Queen of checkers." She opened the chips and placed the bag so they could both reach it easily.

"I appreciate the snacks," he said. "I do not have any to contribute in turn."

Becky gave him a sly look. "Well, I was thinking I could provide the snacks while you provide the weed and we'll call it even."

"The what?"

"The weed. Pot. Mary Jane?"

"I don't have any."

"If you had no pot, you wouldn't need to cover the smell by burning that fat roll of herbs."

"I told you that was for cleansing the room of evil spirits."

"You're just jacking me around," she said.

"No, I'm being serious."

Becky rolled her eyes.

"Are you trying to trick me?" Bjorn asked. "You wrote me up for burning sage last time and now you want me to show you some pot."

Becky uncrossed her legs and stood up. "Christmas is an Aristotelian time," she said.

"What?"

"Aristotle said, 'Who will watch the watchmen?' I'm the watchman and over Christmas break no one is watching me. Everything is according to Becky's rules now. I'll be right back." Becky left, returning a few minutes later with a small plastic baggie and a lighter. "You're killing me here, Unfrid. I'm down to the bottom of my stash. I thought you could help me out." She held a tiny joint with a needle, lit it, took a puff, then offered it to Bjorn.

"No thank you."

"Don't be such a stick in the mud. There's barely enough here to make us lightheaded."

Bjorn didn't consider himself a stick in the mud. Indigenous culture featured mushrooms and other mind-altering herbs but they were used to trigger spiritual journeys, not for recreation. Like most Canadians of Norse descent, he had absorbed many indigenous values through proximity. He looked on such substances with a seriousness akin to how Christians viewed Communion. He expected to use marijuana or mushrooms eventually but had not felt ready for it in the past. But perhaps a small amount with someone more experienced was the best introduction? He took the joint from Becky.

Bjorn inhaled.

"Don't suck in the whole thing," she said as she moved a piece on the board. "That's enough. Leave some for me!"

Bjorn held his breath as long as he could, then exhaled slowly. He moved one of the checkers.

"You have the lung capacity of a deep-sea diver," she said. Play progressed quickly.

By the time Becky jumped Bjorn's last piece, his head felt like it was full of cotton.

"I win," she said. "You suck at this game."

He shrugged. "I was not trying very hard."

"Maybe we should raise the stakes, make it more exciting."

"How could anyone or anything make checkers more exciting?"

"Let's play strip checkers. Each time you jump a piece, the other player takes off a piece of clothing. If you crown one of your pieces you can decide if you want to put something back on or make your opponent take something off."

That seemed like the funniest thing ever to Bjorn.

"You're almost undressed already," said Bjorn. "You're at a disadvantage."

"Well, you're terrible at this game so we're close to even. I get to count my earrings as clothing."

Bjorn shrugged. Only a few moves in and he lost his socks. Becky lost her earrings in a sacrifice that cost Bjorn his flannel shirt. Then he lost his undershirt.

"Are you a bodybuilder?"

"No." Bjorn laughed. He was in a great mood. The weed was not what he expected. He could see things that he normally had to make an effort to see. A bright orange aura surrounded Becky. He also saw a crow perched on his bed, but he was sure that wasn't there in the physical world. The crow cocked an eye at him and cawed.

Bjorn lost his belt. A moment later Becky stood up, reached under her t-shirt, and unfastened a button. She slid her shorts down her legs. "I was wondering if you were wearing anything under that t-shirt," he said.

"You think I walk around bare ass naked?"

"It is less frowned upon to do so in the North," said Bjorn, "but here it is actually practical."

Bjorn discovered that if he gazed into Becky's aura, he could see scenes from her life. He watched her run around as a toddler, screaming and laughing as her daddy chased her around their home. "Cool," said Bjorn.

"What's cool?"

"I'm watching you playing as a little kid."

"Holy shit, you're a lightweight, Bjorn! That little hit shouldn't have done anything to you. And Marijuana doesn't cause hallucinations. You should maybe get your noggin checked." She took another one of his pieces. "Now drop your pants."

Bjorn stood up, unzipped his jeans, and was down to his underwear. In the shadow below the bed, he noticed a gaping mouth filled with circles of needle-like teeth. Apparently, Kev's evil spirit was not gone.

"Now I'm going to see what's under that giant shirt of yours," said Bjorn as he jumped one of Becky's pieces.

"Not yet," she said. "I'm not going to let you see nothing this game." She pulled her arms into her sleeves, reached behind her back and undid her bra. She pushed the bra out through one of the arm holes and popped her arms out again. Behind her, the shadow crept out from under the bed and began to rise, taking on a shape like a cloud of dark gas billowing into the air. The teeth gnashed. The crow cawed a warning and hopped to the other side of the bed. The room seemed ridiculously crowded to Bjorn.

He giggled.

"What's so funny?" Becky asked.

"You didn't have any arms for a second. You were just a big, green t-shirt blob. And now you have arms again."

Becky laughed. "You are a wreck. You're like a baby stoner."

Bjorn laughed again. The shadow with the teeth took a half step toward Becky.

Bjorn jumped one of Becky's pieces and looked at her with as much seriousness as he could muster. "Now the t-shirt..."

"Not yet," she said. She stood up, reached under her shirt, and slid her panties down her legs. They were pink with white hearts on them. She put one finger through a leg hole and twirled them on her finger. The panties flew off and landed on Bjorn's bed. Both of them cracked up.

"I'm getting better at this game," he said. "The only thing you have left to defend your modesty is your shirt."

Becky laughed. "As if I had any modesty! I let you take that piece."

Bjorn scoffed.

"I can prove it," said Becky.

The shadow stood directly behind Becky. A face was coalescing around the gaping mouth. It seethed with anger. "I abjure you to depart, evil spirit," said Bjorn, laughing.

"Fuck you, Unfrid," said Becky.

The spirit did not leave, but as Bjorn and Becky laughed, it roiled in agitation. Bjorn thought this knowledge could be useful.

"Have you ever met someone who does not like laughter?" asked Bjorn.

"Nope," replied Becky as she moved a piece to his side of the board. She crowned it and then retrieved her panties from his bed. "Have you ever met someone who doesn't like laughter?"

"I have," he said, staring at the shadow.

Becky slid her panties back up her legs. She taunted him with a butt wiggle.

"It would have to be a real grump to not like laughter," she said.

"Just what I was thinking," said Bjorn. Each turn, Becky advanced her pieces across the board until she was fully clothed again. Bjorn told jokes while she destroyed him. He watched as the shadow creature recoiled from Becky's laughter.

"You have the worst jokes," she said.

"But you laughed at them."

"I'm high. Everything is funny."

The spirit shrank and receded as they laughed. Finally, it retreated beneath the bed once more.

Becky jumped one of Bjorn's pieces. "Lose the shorts, Viking man!"

Bjorn stood up, dropped his shorts, and stood there completely naked.

Becky looked him up and down. "Merry Christmas to the Queen of Checkers."

"What now?" he asked.

She put the checkers back into the box and scooped it up with the board. "There are no classes tomorrow, Mr. Unfrid, so what's now is that you sleep in." She closed the door behind her, leaving him naked with the empty snack packages and an evil spirit under the bed.

27

"Do you really believe in the Norse gods?" Becky asked Bjorn.

"Most of us believe in the Norse pantheon the way French Catholics believe in God," he replied.

Becky squinted her eyes as if trying to figure out his meaning, but she did not ask any further questions. "Well, among our little group of students we have a Muslim, three Jews, a Hindu, two Buddhists, and whatever you are, so I'm going to re-think the dorm Christmas party."

"You may consider me an agnostic polytheist," said Bjorn.

"How does THAT work?"

"Agnostics feel that deities are ultimately unknowable and—"

"Wait! Wait! Never mind! I'm planning a party, not writing a dissertation. Forget I asked," she said.

On December 24 the remaining students celebrated an all-holiday party. It took place in the dorm basement and appeared to include whatever stuff Becky could find stored in a box somewhere. Decorations included skeletons, a Menorah, four-leaf clover party favors, a flag, red, white and blue streamers, a Christmas tree, plus things Bjorn did not recognize. A classic rock station played on Becky's boombox while Bjorn nibbled on a Halloween cupcake. Sahid, the Palestinian student, was nearby snacking on a bowl of candy hearts.

"I would not eat those," said Bjorn. "Valentine's Day was ten months ago, and you can't be sure those are from this year's holiday."

"Jaw breakers last forever," said Sahid.

"I think they are mints."

Becky had stepped away from the students and perched on the decrepit plaid couch. She scribbled furiously on her clipboard.

Bjorn approached her. He could see she was answering questions on a worksheet. "Why did you bring homework to a holiday party?" Bjorn asked. "And how do you have home-work when there are no classes?"

"It's not homework," said Becky. "I'm applying for an internship at NASA."

"Do you think that's how you become an astronaut?"

"Dummy! I'm not trying to become an astronaut. I want to be a NASA engineer. I want to build space stuff. I figure an internship would really help me out. I grew up in Clear Lake and we have an astronaut in our neighborhood. If he gives me a recommendation it should be easy."

"It's like science fiction," said Bjorn.

Becky scoffed. "Not anymore! Next month NASA is sending a teacher into space. Get that? They're sending up a real, live civilian. Her name is Christa McAuliffe. She will be the first regular person in space, just like me and you." Becky shrugged. "A regular person like me, anyway. After she goes up, it won't be science fiction anymore."

"Is she going to teach alien children?"

Becky kicked Bjorn's shin and directed a frown at him.

"Ow! Are you wearing steel-toed tennis shoes?"

"This is a big deal," Becky said, her voice rising as she spoke. "Civilians going into space means the beginning of human civilization finding its way out there. It's not just experiments from this point on; it's going to become real life that affects all of us. This is the future of our entire race, the moment when the Solar System opens to us. After this it's only a matter of time until we learn to live and work on other worlds. I want to be one of the ones making it happen. I want the future built on my shoulders! And I live in Houston! I'm in the right place at the right time."

Becky gasped for air. She had said everything in a rush and was out of breath.

"That was more passionate than I expected from you," said Bjorn.

"What's that supposed to mean?" she asked, her icy tone warning him to be careful what he said next.

"I just meant… that… you are an RA, and an RA's job is to… curb the passions of… passionate people."

"I hope your major isn't English," she said.

"Why?"

"Because the top skill in that major is bullshitting, and you are no bullshitter."

"What major do I seem like to you?"

"Math or one of the sciences. You're smart enough to be annoying but not clever enough with words to smooth it over."

"Isn't English a default major you take until you decide what you want to do?"

"No."

Bjorn's eyebrows went up. "Oh, of course. About my comment, I'm sorry if I offended you…"

"It's okay," Becky said. "We're still friends. It doesn't bother me to have friends who are so awkward they can't help being asses. I like having the upper hand." She flashed him a smile and leaned his way. "You have no idea how passionate I can be," she said. "I live like I play checkers."

28

"Merry Christmas," said Kev.

The phone receiver was cold against Bjorn's ear and Kev's voice sounded small and far away, but Bjorn felt unexpectedly cheered by the call.

"Happy Yule," said Bjorn.

"What is this Yule stuff?" asked Kev.

"In Canada we don't celebrate Christmas, we celebrate Yule. You Christians added baby Jesus to it and called it Christmas."

"We have Santa Claus," said Kev.

"Santa is a copy of Old Man Winter, a Norse tradition."

"Do you ever stop trying to one-up everyone around you?"

"I don't try," said Bjorn.

Kev sighed on the other end of the line.

"It makes me happy that you called, Kev. If you were here I would go out and buy a goat so we could have a traditional Yule feast with corn and cranberries and fresh loaves of bread!"

"That sounds great, but grocery stores don't sell goat meat in the US."

"That would not be a problem. I could buy a live one and butcher it myself in the Quad courtyard."

"What? No, no Bjorn. Just no. You can't do that."

"I have read the Student Handbook. It is not prohibited. I do not think they would mind at all."

29

Bjorn arrived 15 minutes early to class on the first day of the Spring semester, hoping to catch Irina before she went in. He waited outside the door as the class filled. Even Professor Linsky arrived before Irina. Then he saw her walking to class quickly as if she were trying to catch a bus before it left. She wore black slacks and a black shirt and sunglasses. Her hair had been dyed from brown to black and she seemed as pale as a snowdrift. Her eyes were downcast as if following an invisible trail.

Bjorn's heart fluttered and he felt a rush of excitement at the sight of her. He almost smiled. The feelings caused a moment of confusion. He forced the feelings down and said to himself, *I am just happy to see my friend.*

"How was Christmas break?" he asked.

Irina drew up short and forced her eyes up to his. "Hi Bjorn! I spent a whole month with my mother, so how do you think it went?"

"I'm so sorry," he said. "I wish it had been better. I thought you were going to give me your phone number before you left."

Irina crossed her arms in front of her. "If I had, then you would have called," she said.

"Oh," he said. She had not wanted to talk to him. Maybe she was still mad at him about blowing off their study session before finals.

"If I spoke to you over break, I would have had to explain to my mother why you had my number, and I would have had to tell her all about you."

"That would not bother me."

"You're my friend, Bjorn," she said. "I'm not okay with sharing you with her in any way. I understand if you can't forgive me for cutting you out like that, but I will never ever let my mother know about you, even if it means you don't want to be friends with me anymore."

Bjorn relaxed. Dealing with Irina was so much like dealing with his friends and family back home. "Do not worry," he said. "Pretending I don't exist when your mother is present is the smallest favor I could do for you."

Her lips hinted at a smile. "I'm glad you understand," she said, and headed toward class.

Bjorn put his hand on her arm and stopped her. "I haven't told you yet," he said. "I got a 73 in Russian for first semester. I passed! I could not have done it without you."

Her eyes went wide and she gave him a genuine smile, a kind he had never seen on her face before. "*Ochyen horosho*," she said. "Let's go, we're late." Irina entered class.

Bjorn took one look around before joining her. He felt hope in his heart because he had seen no sign of the Crone following Irina, but then he saw she had been waiting inside the whole time.

30

There was an all-Quad party to start the new semester, and over lunch Anja asked Bjorn if he would like to go. He stuttered so badly he bit his tongue to cover his reaction. She laughed and touched his arm casually. "Oh, you poor thing," she said. He felt her concern as tendrils of heat radiated from her hand, traveling along his arm and all parts of his body. It went into his head and made him woozy and lightheaded. It went to his freshly bitten tongue and made it tingle. It went to his back and shoulders and eased a tension he had not realized he carried. The energy infused his eyes and he began to see auras of those around them and shapes in the distance of minor spirits he usually ignored. Anja wielded an unconscious power. She was a spiritual elephant, a creature whose strength and momentum required no thought or effort.

"Sure, I'll go," Bjorn said. He tried to sound casual but felt both awed and discombobulated. Before he had come to know her, he thought they were alike, but now he knew the Manitou had been correct. He and Anja were not alike. He was grim and dark, while she was bright and energizing. She was the sun, and he the lizard who basked in her glow.

He hoped that what people said about opposites attracting was true.

Anja had class in a few minutes, so she said goodbye and gathered up her tray to leave. The Manitou stayed behind.

"She is more powerful than I realized," Bjorn said to the Manitou. "She is even more powerful than I am."

The Manitou snorted. "There are others on campus more powerful than you, Bjorn, but none to compare to Anja."

"There are others more powerful than me?" he asked. "You are the one who told me I had a rare gift."

"As you do," said the Manitou, "but that is not the same as power."

"I don't understand. I have faced the lamprey-mouthed spirit twice. I made a deal with the Crone and done other things. Anja isn't even sure spirits like that exist. Could she have achieved such accomplishments?"

The Manitou flicked his ear. "For humans, the spirit world is like a big room with the lights off. Many sit in the dark, but even those who seek enlightenment crawl around in the shadows hoping to stumble into a door. If they find a door, they open it so they can go into the next room. That room is just as dark as the first. Masters spend their lives crossing only a few such rooms. But to you, all is illuminated. You walk straight to a door if you want, unlock it, and pass through. There is no limit to what you can learn or how you grow. You, Bjorn, do not need power to be powerful."

31

Besides the sodium lamps that lined almost every path on campus, Houston's metropolitan glow ensured that it was never truly dark, even at night.

"Yes," Bjorn agreed, "there is still a lot of light at night, but I do not think there is enough for this to be a wise decision."

Kev frowned. He held a black plastic disk in his hands. "This is the heaviest one they had," he said. "There wasn't a lot of selection. I won't get enough distance on the long shots if I go with something lighter just because it's more visible."

Bjorn shrugged. "Do not be too disappointed if you lose it," he said. "You should get something easier to find in the dark."

The January night was crisp at 2:20 am. Kev and Bjorn had joined three students from Taub Hall for a game of Frisbee golf. Everyone wore windbreakers and long pants, which in some years was all the consideration Winter received. The tee-off began at the opposite end of the parking lot from the dorm doors, where the park-like area lay between the Quad and Towers. It was a long hole that required heavy discs to make long-distance throws. The disc golf course had 18 targets around campus that had become informally standardized. Most targets were various objets d'art, but a few were fountains or benches or other landmarks. Campus security paid no attention to the nighttime sports, just waved as the disc-wielding students played past them. Bjorn had become addicted to the game and played several nights each week.

Kev was careful and did not lose his disc.

It was near the end of the game when their group came around the Cullen building and Kev nudged Bjorn to get his attention. "What's that woman doing in the pool?" he asked. The fountain and shallow pool in front of the Cullen building was a campus centerpiece, and students were prohibited from going into it. A woman in a light-colored dress walked across the pool. She was luminous in the moonlight.

"You see her?" asked Bjorn.

"I'm not blind!" said Kev. "She's right there. Something is not right about her."

"I wouldn't worry about it," said Bjorn. "Come on, we'll fall behind if we don't keep up."

One of the other students went first, throwing his disc across the water toward the target on the other side. The woman did not even acknowledge the throw even though the disc passed no more than a few yards from her.

"Watch out for pedestrians," said Kev.

The students from Taub looked at him strangely and then took their turns. There were only two more holes after the Cullen fountain hole, so they were back in the dorms before long. It was after three when the two roommates were back in their room, finally exhausted enough to sleep. Bjorn turned off the light and climbed into the top bunk.

Just as Bjorn was about to drift off to sleep, Kev said, "I can't stop thinking about that woman."

"What woman?"

"The woman in the fountain."

Bjorn sighed. "It is really late. I have an essay test first thing in the morning. I probably should not have played disc golf."

"Sure, sure. But I just realized what was wrong with her. Did you notice that she made no waves walking through the fountain?"

"It was dark. You probably just didn't notice them."

"No, no, no. The lamps were reflected in the water. They would have rippled as she walked. She walked all the way across the fountain without making any waves. How could she have done that?"

"How are your nightmares?" asked Bjorn.

"Why? That doesn't have anything to do with the weird woman."

"Just tell me."

"I still get them, but not as often. I had this one dream where I was being eaten alive and you came and gave me a hammer and told me I was in a dream. Ever since then, I always see the hammer when I'm having a nightmare and that reminds me I'm in a dream. Then I stop being afraid. The monster woman screams at me and tries to scare me but she always gets bored when it doesn't work and then she goes away."

"Your friends in the Paranormal Student Association might suggest that your nightmares could be a haunting of sorts and that it opened you psychically to seeing other kinds of hauntings, like perhaps the woman in the fountain."

"I'm being serious here," said Kev.

But Bjorn did not answer. He sighed and drifted into a deep sleep.

32

Bjorn folded clothes in Sett's basement laundry room. He could hear students gathered in the adjacent room, where the All-Holiday Party had taken place. A group of eight students huddled around the AV cart and its giant TV. They had snacks and party hats and noise makers. Bjorn hoped Becky had ditched the remaining candy hearts.

Bjorn half listened as the announcer declared that space shuttle Challenger had lifted off. The students all cheered, Becky the loudest. Bjorn only had time to fold a pair of jeans and a t-shirt before the students fell silent.

"What just happened?" asked one.

Becky screamed.

Bjorn dropped his shirt on the floor and ran into the other room. The students were paralyzed with horror, except for Becky, who sobbed. Bjorn went around to where he could see the screen. At the top of the rocket's trail, the Challenger had been replaced by an expanding ball of gases.

Although he had not followed the shuttle launch, Bjorn was horrified. Instinctively, he reached out with his senses, infiltrating the air that he had tried so many times to master. The Challenger debris was more than 1,500 miles away, but he could feel the acrid chemical vapor and the superheated atoms of the debris. He was there and he was expansive, a consciousness extended across a vast area sensing the winds and tracking the trajectories of every particle of debris. The cockpit was still intact. Inside, the astronauts were alive but terrified and buffeted physically by their uncontrolled fall. Their terror was inside Bjorn, making his heart beat so fast he thought it might rupture.

In desperation, Bjorn gritted his teeth and gathered the strands of moving air, pulling them together into a skein, willing the strands of air to push up, up against the broken cockpit and slow its fall. Sweat broke out on his forehead from the strain.

Tense seconds flitted by, filled with the astronaut's despair and fear pouring into his head until suddenly everything was obliterated by a crushing impact like the hammer of a god.

Bjorn gasped. They were dead.

His body unclenched. He walked over to the kitchenette's sink and threw up into it over and over. He ran cold water, rinsed his mouth and cleaned his face as best he could. His hands shook. Then he walked over to Becky and held her until her sobs died down.

33

The coffee tasted scorched and Bjorn felt scorched inside his head. Anja sat across from him. The Manitou stood nearby, as silent as a statue.

Anja looked at the burger on Bjorn's plate. It had one small bite missing. Bjorn skipped the fries and took a bowl of apple sauce instead, stirring slowly without eating.

"What's going on with you, eh?" she asked.

"I watched the Challenger yesterday."

"That was a tragedy," she said, her face solemn. "I didn't watch it live, but I saw it on the news last night."

"What would you say if I said I felt them die?"

"I'd say you're very empathic, Bjorn."

"I mean that my spirit traveled to them and stayed with them until the moment of their deaths. Everything they thought echoes in my head and everything they felt aches in my heart. I know the last words they wanted to say to their loved ones. I wrote it all down so I wouldn't forget but I don't know how I could ever tell their families about those moments. Even if I could talk to them, they would never believe me and I would only cause them pain. I will have to keep those things to myself, and no one will ever know what the astronauts wanted to say and it is a failure I will carry with me my entire life."

Anja looked alarmed.

"I thought you might be able to understand."

"Stress and grief," she began, "They are intense feelings and sometimes they can be hard for our minds to make sense of. The mind can tell itself stories so that when something happens that we can't understand or accept, we have a way to deal with it."

"Sounds like you got that from psych class."

"I did a whole research paper on delusion and the tricks the mind plays on itself."

Bjorn crossed his arms and began stroking his beard. "Did you, eh?"

"Yes. Is something wrong? You're acting weird. Weirder."

"No, no, just thinking. Why did you pick that subject for a research paper?"

Anja blushed. "I had to pick something."

"But you didn't pick it randomly, right? Something happened that made you want to learn more about that."

Anja crossed her legs and folded her hands in her lap. "That's insightful of you."

"I get hunches about people sometimes."

"Well," she said slowly, not looking into his eyes. "When I was a little girl there was this one summer when I talked every night with my Gran. She would come to me at bedtime and tell me stories about everyone in the family. She made me laugh so much! And she told me all the family secrets and the best gossip."

"That sounds nice," said Bjorn.

"Yes, but it didn't happen. She died in the spring a few months earlier so there is no way I could have spoken to her through the summer. I was just little and couldn't process her death, so I imagined that she came and talked with me."

"All the secrets she told you, were they true?"

Anja shrugged. "Mostly. I'm sure I heard things that I didn't pay attention to consciously. People talk around little kids."

"What was her name, your grandmother?"

"Abedabun."

"If your grandmother's spirit came to visit you right now, would you believe that you did not just imagine her visits when you were little?"

He had never tried this before, but Bjorn repeated the name in his mind, *Abedabun, Abedabun, Abedabun!* He could feel a distant answering recognition but he was too weak to make a solid connection.

"If I saw Gran right now, I would believe that I needed therapy to figure out why I was imagining her again," said Anja.

Bjorn stopped focusing on the name. There was no point in drawing the spirit of Anja's Gran if Anja would not believe it was real. The distant answer fell silent.

The Manitou leaned close to Bjorn. "Do not be disappointed," he said. "That was not the spirit of Abedabun you were calling forth."

34

Kev lounged at his desk, a rare occurrence. He seemed melancholy.

"Is something wrong?" asked Bjorn.

Kev shrugged. "Last night I had a new dream and it was like it was totally real. I thought I woke up and there were astronauts standing in our dorm room dressed in their space suits but with their helmets off. In the dream you were awake and you were talking to them about what it was like to fly."

"So you can see them too."

"You dream about them?"

"I've seen them from time to time since the Challenger exploded."

"I didn't know you were following the space program."

"I connected with the astronauts in their tragedy," said Bjorn, "and now the tragedy haunts me."

35

The last person ahead of him in line finished their business and left. Bjorn moved up to the window. It was the same clerk who had rejected his class selection and made him go through late registration at the beginning of the Fall semester. "I remember you!" she said. She flounced her hair and pulled her Celtic amulet into view.

"So I see," said Bjorn. "I would like to change my major from English to Physics."

"They don't usually go in that direction," she said.

"I thought English was a default major until you decided what you wanted."

"It's not," she said.

"That is what people keep saying."

"Have you filled out the paperwork?"

"No."

She handed him a form. Bjorn took a pen out of his pocket and began filling it out.

"You have to fill it out elsewhere and then go to the back of the line," she said.

Bjorn looked both ways down the hall. It was empty except for him.

Bjorn started to open his mouth but she interrupted. "It's just the way it works, hon."

36

Bjorn scowled as he opened the door. He did not fear the dead but seeing them frequently made him apprehensive. They always became more active when things were about to go to shit, and he had seen too many visitations recently. It felt like something bad was brewing.

A tall man in a three-piece suit and cowboy hat nodded a greeting. He had thin hair, a dimple on the point of his chin, and a chain at his waistcoat that surely belonged to a pocket watch. Bjorn realized he had not heard a knock but had felt the sensation of a knock, like the ghost of a sound.

"I would be obliged if you permitted me to enter," said the man. "I hoped we might talk a spell."

"You didn't need me to open the door for you," said Bjorn.

"I consider myself a man of manners."

Bjorn stepped aside and gestured for him to come in.

The man doffed his hat and inclined slightly at the waist. "Sam, at your disposal." He brushed past Bjorn without so much as a breath of disturbed air before settling in Kev's chair.

Bjorn closed the door and sat in his own chair, turning it around so they faced each other in the small room.

"Your name is *Koga* in Tsalagi, the language of the Cherokee," said Sam. "But there might not be a living soul who could tell you that."

"Cherokee is a lost language," said Bjorn.

Sam nodded. "It is, and that's a great irony if you knew the story."

"I don't believe I've heard it," said Bjorn.

"It would be my pleasure to tell you, if you don't mind me bending your ear for a bit."

"Certainly," said Bjorn, "I'm sure my professor will be very accommodating when I tell him my research paper is late because I had to listen to a strange ghost's story."

"I'm glad he's so understanding," Sam said with a wink. "I count the disappearance of Tsalagi from the earth as one of my chief regrets. I hold myself responsible for its loss. I lived among the Cherokee in Tennessee for three years. My father had passed, and I was looking for direction in my life. A Cherokee chief named Oo-loo-te-ka took me in and treated me as his own son. I even became a Cherokee citizen. But then the white man's world called me back. I served under General Jackson in the war…"

"Which war?"

"The War of 1812. That is why when the decision was made to move the Cherokee out of Tennessee, I was in a position to negotiate a peaceful relocation."

"That was fortunate," said Bjorn.

Sam shook his head slowly. "It's the kind of fortune you never want to have. Can you imagine what it's like to tell your family they must leave their homes or they will be killed? It's luck no one wants, but that's what came to me. There I was trying to decide where the best future for my tribe waited. I had two choices before me: I could arrange for them to go to Arkansas or I could move them into Canada. The Jarland government and the Chippewa culture had hundreds of years of peaceful unity in the north. The choice was clear. The Cherokee, like other tribes before and after them, were welcomed to Canada and integrated peacefully."

"That was fascinating. Thanks for coming," said Bjorn, starting to get up.

Sam motioned for Bjorn to sit back down. "There's more. I met a Cherokee man in 1818 right around the time all of this took place. His name was Sequoya, and he was fascinated with English written words. He didn't speak a bit of English and didn't know how to read or write, but he was determined to bring this knowledge to the Cherokee. He created the Cherokee syllabary. By the time he finished his work, the Cherokee had been relocated to Canada and had begun to adapt to Ojibwe culture. The Chippewa noticed Sequoya's syllabary and recognized its value right off. Sequoya's work was used to create the Ojibwe syllabary. It spread everywhere in Ojibwe culture before the syllabary had a chance to make its mark on Tsalagi. When Sequoya died, his work was lost and Tsalagi was forgotten a few generations later. Sequoya never spoke any language besides Tsalagi, so the man who gave Ojibwe words is known only in silence."

"That was long ago," said Bjorn, "If there is something you left unfinished in life that needs to be done so you can rest…"

"I'm not that kind of spirit," said Sam. "I can't be put to rest by finding a diary or burying a body or some other simple task. I think you'll understand at the end of my tale."

"Okay then," Bjorn said with a huge sigh.

"After a while I ended up down here in Texas same as you. No one here knew my Cherokee name. I was *Kolana*, but everyone called me Sam."

"You introduced yourself as Sam to me. Maybe if you introduced yourself as *Kolana* instead…"

Sam shot Bjorn a sharp look.

"*Kolana* means the Raven. It has powerful significance to

the Cherokee. *Kolana* brings wisdom. The problem with being *Kolana* is that no one needs you unless the choices are hard."

"Like deciding where the Cherokee must go to survive."

"Yes! The Cherokee were strong, so I knew they would survive. But along with that survival would come losses as well. The tough part was deciding what we were willing to lose," said Sam. "The Cherokee gained a home and peace in Canada but lost their culture. After I left the Cherokee, I became the *Kolana* of Texas, even though nobody knew my true name. I ended up leading the Texians in battle against Santa Anna not far from here. We won our freedom because I knew how the Cherokee fought and Santa Anna wasn't prepared for that."

"I think this is all in the syllabus for my history class," said Bjorn.

"All you'll get in that class is facts," said Sam. "I wanted to tell you the why and also the cost."

"Texas was brutal to many people who lived here," said Bjorn. "I'm not sure I want advice from the man who was in charge at the time. It is hard for a Canadian to take a slave holder's discussion of freedom seriously."

"I navigated the waters of my time the best I could, but the currents were strong. I had slaves but I broke the law by educating them. Then I refused to sign for Texas to join the Confederacy and that was the end of me."

"If you had lost the battle to Santa Anna it would have been better for your slaves."

"Now you see," said Sam. "A win can also be a loss."

Bjorn rolled his eyes. "I see you are going to do the 'ghost regrets his actions in life' routine. Since you got the benefit of all your exploitive mistakes during your life, I am not going to pity you for them now."

"It's true my life was full of regrets. That is why I can't be put to rest easily. My restlessness is endless. I made mistakes aplenty. You will too. I was the *Kolana* of Texas. Now you are the *Koga*." Sam stood and fixed Bjorn with a grim stare. "But I didn't come here to find sympathy for my regrets. I came to prepare you for your own."

Sam's cheeks had become sunken and his lips shriveled and skinned back revealing his teeth. His eyes receded in their sockets and his skin thinned and turned dry as paper until his face was just a pale membrane covering the bone of his skull.

"I suppose it was only a matter of time before this conversation turned ominous. But what I want to know, Mr. Houston, is the meaning of the word *Koga*."

But the *Kolana* of Texas disappeared like a bit of fog.

"Odin's balls!" said Bjorn.

37

Bjorn answered the phone on the third ring.

"Is Kev there?"

"No," said Bjorn.

The woman on the other end of the line giggled. "I know he's not there," she said, "because he's here with me. And now you know where he is too, Son of the Crow. He's going to stay with me a long time, too, because you can't turn into a fucking bird out here in the waking world and you don't have a magic hammer in real life. Oh my, Crow, what are you going to do?"

"Sharon? Is that you?"

Sharon hung up.

Bjorn stared at the receiver in his hand for a moment. That had not really been Sharon. The spirit from the Paranormal Student Association headquarters was using Sharon like a puppet. Bjorn had weakened it in this room and in Kev's mind, but in its lair it had been growing stronger in the months since Halloween. Bjorn let his eyes unfocus on the physical world as he tried to pierce deeper into the spirit realm. Under the bed he could see the shadow with the lamprey mouth full of teeth. "You think you're so clever, don't you?" he said to the shadow.

The shadow grinned.

The spirit had waited until almost sundown before calling him. It would be stronger at night, much more dangerous.

"Vikings do not fear the tragedy of their fate," he said to the shadow as he stood to go after Kev. That, he was sure, was something the lamprey had counted on.

Bjorn took his go-bag out of the closet and left the room. Everyone in Bjorn's family had been taught to keep a go-bag in case the worst happened. Bjorn's was a small backpack. It held a flashlight, hunting knife, one day's worth of food, one change of clothes, a small radio, compass, first aid kit, some money and a fake ID. His parents and older siblings' go-bags also held pistols and a box of ammunition. Except for switching out the food periodically, Bjorn had not updated his go-bag in so long that his fake ID showed him as a 12-year-old. He knew that at the bottom of the bag there would still be a super-hero action figure and some fascinating rocks he had collected one summer along a riverbank where one of the tribes had camped each year for centuries. Bjorn didn't stop to dump his child-hood things out; their weight was more comfort than burden. He shouldered the backpack and headed for the stairs.

Outside on the sidewalk, the streetlights had come on. The orange glow of Houston hovered over the horizon as the sun declined. The air was sharp and cold—moist and penetrating. Bjorn took one step toward the edge of campus and a crow landed a few feet away, blocking his path.

"Have you come to help me?" asked Bjorn, but the bird seemed to ignore him as it cocked its head this way and that to keep an eye on its surroundings.

Bjorn took a step toward the bird, but it did not move.

He took another step, then another.

"You have never let me get this close to you," Bjorn said.

"Are we at last friends?" He leaned over to gently stroke the bird's head.

For the first time, the crow looked him directly in the eye. Then it pecked his fingers savagely.

"You little shit!" Bjorn exclaimed. "That's not going to stop me from going to save Kev."

The bird cawed at him, sticking its tongue in his direction as far as it could, then flew off.

Bjorn bandaged his bleeding fingers, then trotted along the sidewalk. He crossed Wheeler Street and left the safety of the campus. He walked barely half a mile and found himself at the house he refused to enter on Halloween. The door was ajar. He pushed it open and peered into the darkness without crossing the threshold.

When he had been here before, there was muted lighting and cute decorations. The house had been shabby but homey and inviting. Now it was silent and dark. A smell of garbage oozed from the door. Bjorn paused to center himself and extend his senses. He could detect the demarcation line of the hallowed ground like a membrane across the door just as he had the first time he had been here. Once he entered the building, he would be in the lamprey's base of power.

Kev had not mentioned the paranormal group since returning from Christmas break and Bjorn had not asked. Things had changed for Kev since the last time Bjorn visited his dreams and delivered Thor's sigil into his hands. Kev reclaimed at least some of his own power, and apparently that had been stronger than the sex drive that drew him to this house. Now Bjorn wished he knew the details of why Kev had written off his little paranormal harem. That knowledge might help him understand why Kev was here now again in the thrall of the lamprey.

But he didn't know, and his ignorance wasn't going to stop him.

Bjorn stepped through the door. A chill ran down his spine

and he felt something bitter on his tongue. The lights did not work. He dug his flashlight out of his go-bag, ignored the stairs going up, and cautiously walked down the hall.

"I know your weakness, Lamprey," Bjorn yelled. "You cannot stand humor or laughter."

Bjorn opened the bathroom door. The sink and the toilet bowl were covered with a black coating. The rugs were rigid with filth and crunchy to step on. Bjorn closed the door.

"They say humor is the best medicine," he continued. "Knock knock?" In the dining room, the table was covered with plates of moldy food, used needles, burned spoons, old candles, and empty prescription bottles. Books and papers were scattered around the floor and the walls were inscribed with runes written with feces. Bjorn covered his nose and mouth with part of his shirt.

"Now you say, 'Who's there?' and I say 'Windigo."

Bjorn moved through the dining room doorway into the kitchen. The counters were filled with empty containers and dirty dishes and pans. Trash lay on the floor. A rat squeaked from an open cupboard.

"And then," Bjorn continued, "you say 'Windigo who?' and I answer 'Windigo home I will be grateful to leave this place. Ha ha. You get it, spirit? You get it? Humor is your weakness. Maybe I should have brought a joke book too."

Adjacent to the kitchen was the living room, a tangle of broken furniture and damp stains. Bjorn could hear moaning through the closed door that undoubtedly led into the master bedroom. He crossed the filthy room and turned the knob. It was moist and sticky.

Bjorn wiped his hand on his pants before going through. "Kev, you better appreciate what I am doing for you."

He opened the door the rest of the way and took a step into the bedroom. A bare mattress lay on the floor. A pair of sickly college students fucked with the doomed persistence of a machine that lacked an off switch. The boy had a slack, empty face and his eyes were white and blind. The girl lay half off the mattress, her boobs jostling every time the boy rammed into her. She turned her blind eyes to Bjorn and mouthed *please help*.

The lamprey spirit was just nasty.

"Mary," Bjorn said. He did not step closer. The couple were both infused with the shadow at the height of its power. He could not dislodge the spirit from them. Perhaps he could give them some respite for a time, however. He took the sage from his pocket and lit one end of it. He waved the smoke around. In his head he heard the lamprey spirit laugh, but she receded to the edges of the room. Mary and the boy slowed, and the boy collapsed on her. They both appeared to have passed out. He set the smoldering sage on a filthy plate that lay on the floor. He had until that was consumed to figure out a more permanent solution. In the meantime, he had to find Kev.

Bjorn left the bedroom and went to the stairs. He climbed them carefully and began checking the upstairs bedrooms. He found Sharon on the second try.

"Where is Kev?" Bjorn asked on entering the room. Sharon sat on the floor in a puddle of her own urine next to a bed, her back against the wall. Like Mary, Sharon was naked. She was skeletal, muscle shrunken, sagging skin draped loosely on her frame, her body covered in sores. Her lips were peeled back from her gums, which had turned black, as had her toes. The air was putrid.

"Where is Kev?" Bjorn asked again.

Sharon lifted one arm to point to the bed beside her where a blanket covered a mound. Bjorn grimaced. He had been afraid that would be the answer. He had to step close to Sharon so he could pull the blanket off the bed. When he did, there was only a pile of trash and clothes. But Sharon grabbed his ankle.

Bjorn found himself pulled into the core of Sharon's being.

It was dark and empty and not at all like the moments he had found himself experiencing Irina's heart and mind. Sharon was a hole, a drain through which her life was pouring like the last bit of water in a bathtub swirling at the bottom. The current pulled at him like a riptide, sucking him down. Sharon was dying and the vacuum was dragging him along.

He tried to pull away from her grip, but he was nearly paralyzed and barely able to move.

"Where are your taunts and bravado now?" asked the lamprey as she walked into the room. "Oh, that's right, that's how you ended up here in the first place."

Bjorn felt himself detaching from the mortal world, losing connection to his body. His sight sharpened and deepened as he slid toward the spirit world. The ceiling and roof had been replaced by the night sky, the moon, and other worlds that the waking eye could not perceive. He saw through the lamprey's hex to her perfect skin and beautiful bone structure, the empty eye sockets, and the nightmare that was her mouth.

With the last of his energy, Bjorn slid his backpack off his shoulders and let it tip over, spilling its contents. He dropped to one knee and put his hand down on a small, brown rock. It was a stone arrowhead. Bjorn pushed his senses into the arrowhead, trying to connect to it and ground himself in the real world.

All around, the bedroom and the whole filthy house were gone. He was on the bank of a river lit only by the moon, at a bend where canoes were drawn up on the shore. He could smell the delicious odor of venison charring over a fire just out of sight. The arrowhead carried the memory of feasting and gratitude for the deer's sacrifice. Bjorn began to feel more solid again.

The lamprey walked through the grasses toward him. "A good trick for a novice," she said. "You might outlast my pawn if I were not here to make you return." She strode up to him and pushed him into the river. Bjorn fell, striking the water with a shock.

He was back in the house, his life pouring into the dying girl. He was down on both knees now, leaning on the edge of the bed.

"Hello!" called a voice from downstairs. "Bjorn, is this the bird that's been following you everywhere? Did you train it to fetch people? Bjorn, are you here?"

"Kev," said Bjorn, but it was barely a whisper.

"Fucking god!" Kev yelled. "What happened to this place? It's like the set of a horror movie starring Cheech and Chong."

Bjorn heard the flapping of wings coming closer and a familiar cawing while someone followed, tromping up the stairs. First the bird and then Kev burst into the room.

"Oh, thank you, Son of the Crow," said the lamprey. "I could not have asked for more!"

"Holy shit! What is that?" said Kev, drawing up short, his eyes fixed on the lamprey spirit. "You're like the monster Cheech and Chong have to kill."

"You can see me in the waking world now!" said the lamprey. "Can you hear me as well? Come to me, Kev. I have missed you dearly."

Kev did not move.

"You're not real! You're not real! You're not real!"

"I am real," she said, "and I am yours to adore and serve!"

Kev shook his head. "No, you're not real. I don't believe it."

The lamprey frowned. "Do not resist, Kev. Come to me now." Bjorn could feel the lamprey exerting her power, trying to put Kev's mind in thrall.

But Kev did not move. The lamprey's power triggered a response in Kev. His eyes glazed over and Bjorn saw that he had fallen into a trance. Kev's hand came up and his fingers traced a rune in the air. It was the rune of Thor that Bjorn had inscribed in his aura as protection. The rune floated in the air, a collection of blue electric arcs. The hair on Bjorn's neck stood on end and the hair that cascaded down his back puffed out with static electricity.

"You're not real," Kev said in his trance state. "You're not real. You're not real."

The lamprey reached out to him but was barred as if by an invisible wall. She turned her scowling face on Bjorn. "You shit on everything I desire, you fucker!" she said.

Like a sleepwalker, Kev moved next to Bjorn and touched his shoulder. Bjorn felt a jolt go through him, energizing his muscles. Bjorn stood and wrenched his foot from Sharon's grasp. The girl turned her face up to Bjorn, and he heard a rattle in her throat. A wisp issued from her lips and rose, disappearing through the ceiling. The girl's husk sagged and toppled over.

The crow landed on Bjorn's shoulder. He shook himself and shambled out of the bedroom with Kev's help. The lamprey screamed with frustration while the crow's caw sounded like a human laugh.

They descended the stairs one step at a time. Bjorn could see Kev's aura. It had grown white and blue and crackled like an electrical storm. Kev was indeed possessed, but not by the likes of the lamprey. Sparks jumped from Bjorn's roommate to the walls as they walked, leaving black spots on the wallpaper. Bjorn's skin tingled with pins and needles as if his whole body had the blood cut off, and now all his nerves were firing as they came back to life. Sparks flew from Kev and singed the carpet.

Outside, Kev seemed to come to himself again. He was disoriented.

"I have to go back," said Bjorn.

"Are you crazy? Something is wrong here," said his roommate. "I'm having trouble remembering. It's like a dream, but

I think I saw Sharon in there. I don't think she's alive anymore."

"Sharon is dead. But Mary and some guy are in the master bedroom. I have to get them out."

Bjorn could barely move on his own. Kev left him, dashing through the door to return a few minutes later with Mary. Thin smoke was coming from the smoldering carpet. Kev laid Mary on the grass and darted inside again. When he returned carrying Mary's unconscious companion, Kev had to dodge around small fires that sprang up and danced like pagans.

Flames showed through the windows in minutes. Sirens heralded the arrival of the fire department and ambulances. Mary and the boy were taken to the hospital. A police officer wanted to take Bjorn and Kev's statements.

"They're in shock," the paramedic told the officer. "They're mumbling gibberish."

Paramedics took Bjorn and Kev to the hospital. When they were cleared by the doctors, they were taken to the police station where they were questioned until late into the night. Finally, the officer leaned back and sighed. "I'm going to book you both for drugs," he said. "You are clearly high as a kite."

But they had barely begun booking the two into the system when another detective approached. "Cut them loose," he said.

Bjorn was as confused as the booking officer until he and Kev walked out of the station's lobby and Bjorn saw the stocky man in the loose pants, the black sports jacket, and the blonde ponytail. The man's stubbly cheeks lifted in a grin that showed perfect teeth.

"Just in the nick," the man said. "Almost like fate, eh little brother?"

38

Still a few hours before dawn and the diner was packed as if it were the lunch rush. Bjorn, Kev, and Bjorn's brother Ivar sat below the glaring light at one of the small, white-topped tables in the nonsmoking section of the restaurant, which was separated from the smoking section by little more than good intentions. Bjorn's eyes watered from the drifting smoke coming from the after-hours club crowd that lingered over coffee and dessert and cigarettes waiting for their blood alcohol levels to descend to legal limits.

"Drink your hot chocolates," said Ivar.

"I think I'd prefer something with alcohol in it," said Kev. "Or something else that promotes forgetfulness or something. Because tonight was like I was in a dream but I know it wasn't but it can't have been real."

"Chocolate is very grounding," said Bjorn.

"It is," said Ivar.

"How did you show up like that?" Kev asked Ivar. "You came out of nowhere. It was like magic."

Ivar chuckled. "Just serendipity."

"Serendipity is a force," said Bjorn.

"I have a nose for trouble," continued Ivar, tapping his nose with one finger. "I landed at the airport today. I had to come to town for business. I was planning to catch up with Bjorn when I was finished, maybe take a day and go to Astroworld together or some shit. But as soon as I got off the plane I smelled something I have not smelled in years. When Bjorn was little he would only wash his hair with shampoo that had his favorite superhero on it. It was just a strawberry shampoo, but it was cheap and did not smell like real strawberries. Nothing else smells like it and I could not stop smelling it. So after I rented a car and got settled at my hotel, I came to find my brother. By then it was late and your RA threatened to call security on me."

"That would be Becky."

"Before she could do that, one of your neighbors came to see what was going on. She is a junior and she writes for the Daily Cougar. She was staying up late working on a story about the fire because it was right by campus and involved a student organization. She was excited that her neighbors had been there and was watching out her door to see if she could catch you coming home. She asked me lots of questions. She is the one who told me what happened. After that I just had to make some calls to hospitals and police stations."

"How did you get us out so fast?" asked Kev. "And without a lawyer?"

"I always carry hundreds of dollars of get-out-of-jail-free cards with me when I travel for business."

"If it was hundreds of dollars," said Kev, "then they wouldn't be free because, you know, money isn't free. That's sort of what makes it money, right? It's the idea nothing's free or we wouldn't need money."

"If you're in the right profession, you can get your money for nothing," said Ivar.

"You mean you're a rock star?" asked Kev.

"What?"

"It's a line from a song," explained Bjorn.

"I'm a little out of touch with anything that isn't Viking metal," admitted Ivar.

"If Bjorn is explaining pop-culture references to you, you're lots and lots out of touch. Like somebody's 98-year-old grandfather who lives out in the woods in a cabin and never got electricity or indoor plumbing."

"Just drink your hot chocolate," said Ivar.

Kev took a sip of the brown beverage. "You bribed a cop. That seems dangerous."

"I wouldn't recommend trying it yourself," said Ivar. "You have to know how to spot the ones who are likely to go for it, and you have to know how to make an offer without making an offer."

"If you're not a rock star, what exactly do you do for your family's business, Ivar?" asked Kev.

"I'm a fixer."

"What do you fix?"

"You might also call me a troubleshooter."

"What do you sh—" Kev began, but Bjorn gave a small shake of his head and Kev dropped it. "I think I need to visit the bathroom." Bjorn stood so Kev could slide out of the tiny booth.

"That is a lot of serendipity showing up just as we needed you," said Bjorn when he had seated himself again. "You have the Sight, don't you?"

"More like the nose. But I've never let Dad know. This is the first time I've ever told anyone because I didn't want it getting back to him. He still hassles Mom for dabbling in these things. I figure it's safe enough to talk about it down here in Hell's lobby."

"You would never hear the end of it if he found out you were sensitive," said Bjorn. "He can't tolerate the thought of something existing if you can't weigh it, measure it, or take a photo of it."

"You have the Sight, right?" asked Ivar. "That's why you asked me."

Bjorn nodded. "I've never told anyone either. I'm sure Mom has figured it out."

"She knows all the secrets, usually before you tell her."

"How convenient it would be if Dad were so open-minded," said Bjorn.

"Have some compassion for the Old Man. Mom told me why he's like that. She says he used to have the Sight. He was a seer, but the path was too much. He spent some time in a sanitorium back when that was worse than prison. To get his freedom he had to admit his visions were hallucinations. Eventually he believed it. The Sight goes away if it is denied long enough. He thinks he survived insanity, so I guess he is afraid we might be prone to losing our minds as well."

"That's why he's so sour these days, I suppose," said Bjorn.

Ivar nodded. "Deny yourself and that's what you get."

The waiter brought Ivar his slice of French Blackbottom Pie. "Don't you two make the darling blonde bookends?"

"We're brothers," said Ivar with a grin. "I'm on my own. And I decide who I'm bookends with."

"Best tip I've had all night," said the waiter as he gave Ivar an over-the-shoulder smile and a wink while walking away.

"You're very friendly with the staff," said Bjorn. "You know this is the Montrose district. They say all the waitstaff in this restaurant are gay."

"Oh my goodness, I would never have known! Thank you, little brother!" exclaimed Ivar, one hand held over his heart in surprise.

"Shut up!" said Bjorn, feeling the heat of embarrassment rising in his cheeks.

"I love your subtlety!"

"I see how things are," said Bjorn. "Are you like Dad? Do you deny yourself?"

Ivar took a huge bite of the French Blackbottom and cast a glance at the waiter. "I deny myself nothing!"

39

Bjorn shrugged off his sense of foreboding, walking quickly back from PGH after finishing his last class of the week. Apprehension stalked him. He assumed he had the jitters because it was the night of the party Anja had invited him to. He was so close to the relationship he dreamed of having with her that just thinking about it made his palms sweaty and the back of his throat dry. He knew that she liked him, and they had come close to getting together before Christmas break. He was at once optimistic about what this party would mean for them and nervous that he might screw it up.

Almost back to Settegast, Bjorn saw the Crone. She stood in front of Taub Hall, one arm extended and elevated like an hour hand pointing at two o'clock. He could feel the prickling of the hairs on his neck. This was where his real apprehension had come from, a premonition of bad news. Bjorn slowed, reluctant to talk to her.

"This is the first time you have come to me," said Bjorn.

"It is the darkest point," said the Crone. "This is the time I said I would come."

"Must it be tonight?"

"No," said the Crone. "Averting Irina's doom is your decision. You may choose to leave her to her fate."

"I don't have a key to Taub."

"The door will open to you."

"And I don't know her room number. I've never been to her room before. We always studied someplace else."

"It is 336."

Bjorn nodded and strode up the short flight of steps to the door. As he approached, a pair of laughing students exited the building. Bjorn caught the door before it could close and went in. He climbed the stairs to the third floor. Taub was shaped like the capital letter T and he was at one end of the top. He went down the hall until he could turn down the center line. Irina would be near the end.

A shiver went down his spine as he passed a door along the way. He stopped. The room was 326. He heard the words *"The time is not yet"* in his mind. He moved on until he found 336. Without hesitating he rapped on the door.

A moment later Irina opened it.

"Oh!" she said. "What are you doing here?"

Bjorn wondered the same thing.

"I was thinking about you," he said. "I haven't seen much of you lately."

"I didn't forget you, Bjorn. I was planning to ask you if you want to study before the test, but we have a whole week. I was hoping we could make MacGyver night into a regular thing too."

Bjorn shrugged. "Sure, I'd like that."

"Well?" she asked.

"Well what?"

"Are you just going to stand in the hallway?"

"What?"

Irina grabbed his shirt and pulled him into the room. "Sometimes you are such a little boy!" she said affectionately.

Her roommate was out. The desks were tidy. One was clear except for a lamp while the other held pink organizers with pens and pencils and erasers and paperclips. One of the beds had a matching pink bedspread with a design of white hair bows. The other bed was unmade, with blue sheets and a soft, brown blanket on top.

Bjorn pointed at the blue and brown tangle. "Is that one yours?"

Irina shook her head.

He studied the smartly made bed. "There is more pink than I expected," he said.

Wordlessly she strode to the closet and opened the door. Inside, more than a dozen dresses in several shades of pink hung from the bar. Pink shoes were lined up below the dresses. "This is where I keep the clothes I don't wear," she said. "Except for when I'm home and my mother makes me. She insists pink is my color."

Irina was open to him. It was not like the first time he felt drawn into her heart by a momentary intense emotion that she felt. These days it was constant whenever he was with her. She was simply open to him all the time in a way no one else ever had been. It felt like pure trust. He hoped to live up to her faith in him.

In the hard, dark place buried deep in Irina's soul, Bjorn felt something new. She was at peace. He experienced momentary relief that the persistent sour ache was gone, but he was suspicious of unforeseen happy resolutions. He expected Irina was the sort of person who must go through trials of fire to emerge tempered and sharp edged. Her wounds were too deep for her to change her mind so easily. This was not right. Something was not right.

"Fuck your mom!" he said, hoping to provoke her and maybe get a clue to what was going on.

Irina laughed. "What?"

"Fuck her pink dresses! You should burn them."

"That's not necessary," she said, her voice drab and lacking energy. "It wouldn't do anything. It wouldn't matter."

Something was definitely wrong with her. She was like a limp dish rag. Maybe he needed to provoke her more. Bjorn stepped into the closet and grabbed the closest pink dress. He tossed the hanger to the floor and tried to pull the dress in half. His muscles strained and his face turned bright red. He huffed and puffed. The dress was very sturdy. The seconds stretched out.

"That is a $200 dress," she said, not sounding upset at all.

"It is a $200 chain around your neck!" he said. The fabric let out a ripping sound and it began splitting apart. It was easier then. After the first rip, there were plenty of weak points in the fabric that he could tear.

Deep in Irina's mind he heard the words *It won't matter soon anyway*. She reached past him and grabbed the next dress. Knowing the dress's vulnerable point, she had an easier time shredding it. Soon, the two dresses were just heaps of cloth strips on the floor. Bjorn grabbed the next dress and Irina the one after that.

When all the pink dresses had been destroyed, the pair were sweaty and breathing hard. Irina was grinning. She led him out of the closet and they both sat on the floor. Bjorn wondered what he had accomplished.

"That was very rebellious," she said. "But it felt good. Fuck my mom!"

"You are a rebellious person."

"Not openly. I don't say the things I want to say and I don't do the things I want to do. You only know me here where my mother can't see what I'm doing."

"Then you should say what you think and do what you want to do."

Irina laughed. "You make it sound so simple! Bjorn, have you ever seen how a slaughterhouse works?"

"I have seen animals slaughtered on a farm before."

"It's different in a slaughterhouse. The cattle come out of the truck and they move single file along a fenced path into the slaughterhouse. They don't get to choose their path and then they die so someone else can eat a burger with fries. It's no life for them and they get no say. Their fate is determined. That's how my life is. It would be better for the cow if she could at least pick the moment she dies."

So that was it, thought Bjorn. "You think this hypothetical cow should kill herself?" he asked.

"If she wants to be in control of her own life, maybe she needs to."

Now Bjorn understood her peace. It was resignation. She was done with the life that had been dictated to her and she had decided to exert her will in the only way she knew how. She was going to end it all. Irina's whole life pointed to this moment, and the Crone had given him five minutes warning to avert nineteen years of momentum. He couldn't turn that around.

Maybe he could give Irina one more day.

"If the cow believed she was going to die, maybe she would be more daring since she had nothing to lose," he said. "Maybe then she could make choices she had not considered."

"It's just a cow," she said. "She lives boxed in by fences."

"It's a metaphor with a hypothetical cow. If we want, she can kick down the fence and go running across a field and eat wildflowers for the first time in her life. Now, what if you were that cow," he said, "and you knew you were going to die? What would you do that you had been afraid to do before, something that would be worth living another day for?"

Irina wrinkled her brows in thought. "I'm not really afraid…"

"But you stop yourself from doing things. What if, at the

end of everything, your inhibitions were gone and nothing is off limits?"

As Irina considered the question, he could feel her unconscious barriers melt away until her buried desires revealed themselves. He was so connected in that moment that he could hear her thoughts.

Change my major…

Visit the Loire Valley…

Gorge on dark chocolate…

Smash a car to pieces with a baseball bat…

Burn my mother's house down…

…With her yappy dog inside it…

But there were no thoughts and no words to warn him before she grabbed his shirt for the second time and pulled him close. Her lips were soft and yearning against his, her hands and arms roaming like the hands of a blind person discovering the shape of their world.

The dark, cold place in Irina's heart thawed. Below the accretion of years of disappointment and loneliness stirred forbidden things: hope and desire. Her hunger became his hunger and he warmed himself at the fire of her passion. In his own way, Bjorn had suffered lifelong isolation just as she had. He understood this woman and was beginning to realize how precious she was to him. He had not wanted this, but it was happening, and in this moment Irina was all he desired.

But it felt like deceit. Irina did not know Anja was in his heart. If this is what she needed to avert her doom and he was doing this to keep her alive, then wasn't he just manipulating her? And what was he feeling toward Irina anyway?

I love her, he thought.

His heart fluttered in panic. This was not the love he dreamed of.

Bjorn pulled away enough to speak. "Irina, this is… this may be a mistake. It is probably a mistake."

She nodded, inches from his face. "A terrible, horrible mistake," she agreed. "I have waited my whole life to make a huge, dreadful mistake. I'm so glad it has finally arrived. This is the awful mistake I want to make, while there's time. One day you can tell the story of what a stupid idiot you were and how much wiser you have become. But at least it was great at the time. Doesn't everyone deserve something worth regretting?"

His heart raced and he had become so hard that it felt like his cock had been folded in half and broken in the process. "Yes," he said, "I really want to make the most foolish mistake of my life."

Irina grabbed his shirt, pulled it over his head and threw it across the room to land on her desk. They tugged and pulled at each other's clothes until their garments were scattered everywhere, then they tumbled into the bed and he was inside her, both of them moving in synchrony as if they had been lovers for years.

When they finished, they lay in an exhausted tangle for a little while. Irina recovered first and ran her fingertips across his skin, making him tingle until he had to have her again.

The third time, she was on top, telling him what to do while her nipples brushed back and forth on his chest. She played with his hair and whispered throughout, telling him stories about the things she wanted as a child, the things she had given up on, and how her world had become smaller each time.

After that he had no more in him for sex, so they used hands and tongues and even some toys that Irina kept hidden in the suitcase stowed below her bed. When that was done, she fell into an exhausted sleep nestled up to him like the cover of a smutty romance novel. He looked at her as she drooled on his chest and his own heart was open and full to overflowing with a terrifying love. He knew Irina. It was like he had always known her. Perhaps they had been together in past lives, a pair of dark hearts comforted in the shadows only by the presence of the other.

At this exact moment, Anja would be in her room asleep by now, the bright light of his life. This new love was choking out his hope and his dreams. "What have I done?" he whispered, knowing that whatever happened next would break his heart.

40

Bjorn could not look Anja in the eye.

"What's wrong with you today?" she asked. "I can tell when something's bothering you because you don't eat." Her plate was loaded with scrambled eggs and toast. She spread ketchup liberally over the eggs. Bjorn sipped a coffee and nibbled a piece of toast.

"Have you ever made a huge mistake and you were sure you would do it again?" he asked.

"I have a few very bad friends," she said. "But they are good people. Once or twice I've done some stuff I could've got in trouble for because I went along with them. I probably have some more mistakes in my future. Is that what you mean?" Anja laughed a little.

"Are you afraid they will change you?" he asked. "Make your life something you did not want?"

"Maybe I'll change them," she said.

"You can't expect to change people," said Bjorn. "They have to want to change themselves, and even then it is not likely."

"Perhaps you don't understand what it means to be a holy woman," said the Manitou from a few feet away.

"I believe most people want their lives to get better. Sometimes all they need is to have the right influences around them," said Anja. "I try to be that for them. What's this mistake that's got you down today?"

Bjorn sighed and looked bleak but said nothing.

Anja waited a few beats before speaking again. "It's private. I understand. Maybe you should have come to the party instead."

"A situation arose…"

"I was looking forward to seeing you there."

He finally looked into her eyes. "If you really knew me…"

"I think I do. You're noble and selfless and the most honest person I've met."

Bjorn's throat choked up. He didn't deserve those kind words.

"And because of that, I have a confession to make." Now she averted her eyes, studying her eggs as she ate them, a self-conscious smile plumping her cheeks like sweet muffins.

"What kind of confession could you have to make?"

"I'm going to confess my own ugly character flaw that I have hidden my whole life and when you hear it you're going to understand why I'm telling you now. Before I tell you, I want to remind you I'm a Leo."

"What has that got to do with anything?"

"People expect Leos to act like kings and queens and get the glory. I would like to think I'm not like that but I kind of am. I'd rather think it's part of being a Leo so it's not entirely my fault." She laughed a little and he almost laughed with her. "The thing is that everyone always wants me for a friend, but it usually doesn't work out. I feel like I'm talking down to people most of the time. It's hard to build a friendship on that because it's like everyone is following me or below me looking up."

"I don't get that impression from you."

"I try to hide it. And I don't mean I'm smarter than

everyone else because I'm not. It's hard to explain. It's like I understand the world better than other people and know what's going on. Nobody understands what I understand. It's a barrier between me and them. I don't get that feeling around you. I relax when we're together. And I was thinking maybe we could try being together."

"Together?" he said as if he had never heard the word before.

"Yeah, together. Like you and me."

Bjorn stared.

"Don't leave me hanging! I've never done this before!"

41

Bjorn knocked on Irina's door. He was supposed to come by her room to study Russian from seven to eight, but his new plan was to tell her their mistake was in truth a mistake and that he had to break it off. His heart raced and his body prepared itself for the encounter in its own way by becoming hard. It's not what he would have chosen if his body had given him a say in the matter.

"*Zdrastvoyte,*" said Irina when she opened the door. She wore a short black skirt and a black tank top with a gold chain that ended in a skull pendant. She looked down at his tented pants.

"Oh! You are so ridiculous! Don't stand in the hallway like that! Get in here!" She pulled him into the room and threw her arms around him as the door slammed shut.

"Irina! Irina!" he said, trying to disentangle himself. His stomach churned and became hot. He could feel energy flowing from him to her and back again, a circuit of connection and intimacy. He could feel her heartbeat in the pulse below her skin. His own heart fluttered, matching her rhythm, synchronizing with hers. "Irina, I have to tell you something."

"I know, baby, I know," she whispered into his neck. "We're making a terrible mistake. This is wrong and a bad idea. I should have worn underwear under this skirt, but I didn't and that just keeps the mistakes going." Then her mouth was on his and her hand moved his hand under her skirt and moments later neither one of them was wearing a stitch except for the gold chain with the skull pendant.

At 9:30 they stopped what they were doing and lay still. Slowly, Irina began quizzing him.

"Shto eta?"

"Kak dyela?"

"Panemaetse pa-Rusky?"

She stopped after a while. "You got them all right, lover," she said. "And your pronunciation is improving."

He didn't answer. There was no way to explain that he was more comfortable with Russian since the Crone put her hand on his shoulder.

"We need to stop seeing each other," he said.

"We are two people clinging together while the boat is sinking," said Irina. "This can't be the love it feels like. I will break your heart and you will shatter mine and all our lives we will carry the scars of fucking up something that is too good to be true. You're right; we should break up." Then she snuggled tighter to him. "Let's break up in the morning," she said, and fell asleep.

42

The library smelled of old paper, that stuffy, heady odor that brings drowsiness. Bjorn was alone on the third floor. It was a drizzly, damp evening near closing time. Few students lingered. He found a small table and made himself comfortable. He took the brown arrowhead out of his backpack and set it on the table.

"Manitou," he whispered, and the Manitou appeared.

"That arrowhead was the work of Morning Thunderhead," said the Manitou, "a great hunter who was angry at the sun for waking him every morning. When he died, his son used that same arrowhead for many years."

"It may have saved my life," said Bjorn. "The lamprey spirit set a trap for me and almost pulled me to the other side. This arrowhead rooted me in this world. The crow helped too."

"The arrowhead belongs beside the river where it can dream of hunting and feasting."

"I will put it back when I return to Canada," promised Bjorn. "But I made an oath not to go back until I could claim my family legacy by learning how to fly."

"Being the son of the crow does not make you a real bird," said the Manitou.

"My grandfather did it," Bjorn said, "and I have an affinity for the air. I can reach out with my mind and feel the air like it's another hand. I just haven't learned to control it. When the shuttle exploded I was there, one with the atmosphere. I tried to save the astronauts but I wasn't strong enough, so I'm practicing to get stronger."

"The air will never be your hand," said the Manitou. "What you feel is not fingers but lines of possibility."

"I don't understand."

"Become one with the air."

Bjorn inhaled. As he let it out, his mind followed the breath, expanding beyond his body.

"How does it feel?" asked the Manitou.

"I feel a thousand tendrils spreading out from me like a catfish's whiskers."

"They aren't currents of air or fingers you can wiggle. They are things that might be."

"Things like what?"

"Like the possibility an updraft will save you when you jump out of a plane like your grandfather. It is a thin chance. Over time you increase the possibility of the thing you want until it happens. Call to the air now and ask it to help you fly. Don't tell it how. Let it choose the way."

Bjorn closed his eyes. "Come to me, power of flight." He opened his eyes. "This feels ridiculous."

"Only because you ask for ridiculous things."

It did not seem ridiculous for long. He could feel a change.

"You feel that?" asked the Manitou. "That is you planting a seed. Call to it regularly and the possibility will become a certainty. At that moment it will be time to harvest your dream."

Then the spirits of the astronauts stood next to him. Bjorn

saw his own face reflected in their mirrored helmets. He heard an astronaut's voice, staticky and rough as if coming over a radio. "It's in the wind," said the voice. Exactly what was in the wind Bjorn would not learn because as abruptly as the spirits of the astronauts appeared, they vanished.

43

The steakhouse was laid out inside like an 1800's restaurant and show hall. A woman with a hoop skirt sat on a trapeze and swung over the stage. The walls were red trimmed with gold.

"Thanks for bringing me along," said Kev.

Ivar gave him a grin. "It's a tradition for parents to take their kid's roommate out to eat at the beginning of the school year. Our parents are never coming down here so I'm going to sub in for a second semester dinner. It's not a big deal. I'm going to expense it."

Ivar had "Viking boardroom hair." It was just long enough to brush the top of his shoulders and was considered respectable for business settings in Canada. Sometimes he wore it in a short ponytail. He was dressed in a black suit as if he were going to a funeral, but he had taken his jacket off and left it in the coat check when they came in. He had a white, pressed shirt that barely contained his barrel chest and beefy arms. Their steaks were extra thick, seared and crusty on the outside, pink and juicy and flavorful on the inside. A basket of fresh out-of-the-oven rolls had been put in the center of the table while off to one side a huge block of aged Swiss cheese sat on a wooden cutting board with a cheese slicer. The food was at once simple yet extravagant.

"I'm surprised you're still here," said Bjorn.

"Me too," said Ivar. "But once in a while tracking down loose ends takes longer than expected. I'll be here as long as I need to be to deal with all the details. This dinner out could be a weekly thing. It's been a long time since we've been able to hang out, little brother. What do you think?"

"I'd like that."

"Is that… is that a bandage?" asked Kev. Kev's eyes were on a bit of medical tape showing on Ivar's neck now that he had loosened his tie and undone the top two buttons of his shirt. There was a slight bulge over his right shoulder.

"That?" asked Ivar. "That's nothing, just a flesh wound."

"I don't think you mean flesh wound," said Bjorn. "People frequently associate 'flesh wound' with injuries by gunfire. And you couldn't mean that because why would you be involved in something like that? Right?"

"Oh, right! No, no, by *flesh wound* I mean minor injury. I walked under a tree and it had a broken branch. Went right in my shoulder. Freak accident but very minor."

"A tree branch?" asked Kev.

"Sure. That's a perfectly plausible explanation."

"Right," said Kev.

"I was not suggesting you elaborate on your injury," said Bjorn. "Just choose more neutral words. And say less. Less is more."

"Less is indeed more," agreed Ivar. "And this was not a big deal. It bled a lot but sometimes minor injuries can bleed the most. My shirt was ruined, the whole thing as red as if I was a butcher. You would have thought I was going to die."

"Less," said Bjorn.

"It's okay," said Ivar with a wink. "I might have looked

awful, but when it was done you should have seen the other guy!"

"Other guy?" asked Kev.

"By 'other guy' I mean tree. What else would I mean?"

44

Bjorn could sense the Crone before he saw her.

"You've come to collect your favor," said Bjorn.

"Soon," she said, nodding.

"You told me I would pay my own price for averting Irina's doom," said Bjorn.

"You have begun those payments already," said the Crone.

"Then how do I owe you this favor?"

"You asked if I would help you," she said, "and that is a covenant of intervention. For me to intervene on your behalf you must agree to intervene on my behalf."

"You're a Major Arcana, a powerful spirit," said Bjorn. "What do you need me for?"

"You just answered your own question. I'm a spirit. My kind have limits. From time to time we need agents who can work for us in the physical world more directly than we can ourselves. And sometimes we do not need such agents. Some humans have gone their whole lives without being asked to return their favor."

"But me you ask right away," said Bjorn with a sigh.

"You have qualities that make you more valuable as an agent than other mortals," said the Crone.

"The gift of Sight. I know."

"No," said the Crone, "Your soul is very old. It is inter-woven with ancient traditions. Regard this cord." She lifted one robed arm. In her hand she held a silver cord glistening in the light as if it were liquid metal. The cord spilled onto the floor and led to his foot, where it blended into his own aura. He shook his foot but it did not come loose.

"I have never seen this before."

"The spirit world is highly metaphorical," said the Crone. "Some metaphors can only be seen when they are used."

The cord connected Bjorn to the Crone. He scowled in apprehension. He did not feel comfortable being bound to a spirit with a magic rope.

"This is the binding between us, favor to favor, connecting word to life. Breaking it would have catastrophic conse-quences for you in this life and the next. Some would struggle against it, performing their service only under threat of the consequences. But I know you, Bjorn. Deep in your soul you feel the obligation as a *weird*."

"I'm not Scottish."

"Vikings also believe in destiny," she said.

"Destiny is just a destination. I can choose the path I take to get there."

"Exactly!" she said. "And you will always choose to face your destiny with bravery and honor. I don't need this cord to bind you, Bjorn, because you will not shy from fulfilling it no matter what it is or what it costs you."

"That sounds like a tragedy waiting to happen."

The Crone shrugged. "Honor and Tragedy are incestuous lovers," she said.

"What must I do?"

"The negotiation has been struck but the time has not come."

"The negotiation?"

"In the spirit world we also make deals with one another.

Another Power has petitioned me for intercession with their follower and you shall be the instrument in their salvation."

"I don't want to be anyone's savior, but if I'm saving someone it doesn't sound as awful as I expected," said Bjorn. "I'm sure it will take a turn for the worse though."

45

Professor Maxwell walked around the room handing back papers. Bjorn's analysis of Oedipus Rex had a great big A minus circled at the top. The grade was much better than he had expected. He flipped through the pages. There was some red here and there but mostly commentary, not corrections.

"I liked the line about Honor and Tragedy being incestuous lovers," said Professor Maxwell. "It's a touch too poetic, almost purple prose. But it's a solid way to make a point while returning to the greater literary themes. On the other hand, I don't expect a freshman to come up with lines like that. Since you didn't list a citation for wherever you got it, I gave you an A minus instead of an A."

"Probably would have gotten a worse grade if I had given the proper citation," muttered Bjorn under his breath.

46

In Houston, February was a month that showed abrupt and wide mood swings, sometimes cold and petty, sometimes cheerful and warm, sometimes rainy and sad, sometimes dry and contemplative. The month was growing more cheerful as it passed toward March. On a Saturday afternoon, Bjorn stood on the fringe of a small crowd gathered in the park-like area between Towers and the Quad where a band played an open-air concert arranged by one of the student organizations. He couldn't follow the song lyrics because his entire focus was on Irina's hand, her fingers interlaced with his, her grip warm and firm and confident. She swayed while he stood stiff and awkward, not sure if he, Irina, or the Crone had chosen this.

The Crone stood nearby. Bjorn noted her toe tapping to the music. He would not have thought the Crone would be into pop music.

In the crowd he saw the Manitou.

"Fuck me!" said Bjorn. And then Anja was in front of him.

"Bjorn! Where have you been? I've missed you. Did I do something wrong?" Then Anja's eyes followed his arm down to where his hand was clasped to Irina's. They followed Irina's arm up to her face with the dark eyes and dark hair and full lips. The women's gazes locked together. "Oh!" said Anja. "That's why you ditched me!"

"Ditched you?" Irina asked Anja. She turned her head to Bjorn. "Were you with this woman?"

Bjorn did not speak.

Irina turned to Anja. "I didn't know he was dating anyone!"

"Neither did I!" said Anja.

"It has been very confusing for me as well," said Bjorn.

"He is the soul of honesty," said the Manitou.

"But has clothed himself as king of liars!" finished the Crone.

"I did not mean for anything like this to happen!" said Bjorn, wishing the women could hear the words of the spirits.

Anja's face began to crack and a big, fat tear rolled out of one eye and down her cheek. "I felt like I could trust you," she said. "I'm never wrong! How could you fool me this way?"

"He is the most trustworthy person you know," said the Manitou, "but trust and safety and comfort are not to be yours, Anja. It takes a crucible to make iron into steel. One day you shall be the spearhead of your people!"

"I'm surprised too, Bjorn," said Irina. "I mean, you told me what we were doing was wrong but I didn't think it would be wrong because you were cheating on me. Or her. Us." Irina shook his hand off and crossed her arms. "Did you really feel anything at all or were you just getting off on sleeping with two women at the same time?"

"I never slept with him!" said Anja.

"That's a surprise now that I know everything. He has a huge appetite for sex. I could see him needing two women to get enough."

"What?" asked Bjorn. "Why would you say that? You don't know everything! There is so much you don't know!"

"What do you mean I don't know everything?" asked Irina. "Is there someone else we don't know about?"

Bjorn looked from the Crone to the Manitou, but of course he could not explain anything about them.

"I came to tell you it is time for you to fulfill your favor," said the Crone. "It's better if you just leave."

The crow landed on his shoulder and pecked his ear. He brushed the bird off and it rose into the air with a squawk.

"Even the fucking bird is against you," said Irina.

The crow cawed at Irina and flew off in the direction of the dorms.

"A life hangs in the balance," said the Crone. "You must not hesitate. The crow will guide you."

"I better go," said Bjorn.

"Running off? You need to learn to face your own shit, Bjorn!" said Anja.

Bjorn left, his face red with shame. His last sight of Irina and Anja was the two women, their faces filled with rage and hurt. They stood close and spoke fast but he could not tell if their angry words were about him or each other.

At the dorms, Bjorn ran up the stairs to Settegast's second floor. He raced to his door and burst through, hoping to find Kev.

"Are your pants on fire?" asked his roommate.

"Can you give me a ride? Right now?"

"Yeah, sure," said Kev. "I'm only working on my major project for history class."

"I'm sorry," said Bjorn. "Never mind."

"Don't let it bother you," said Kev. "Let's go. I'd do anything you want to procrastinate another day. It's like 20% of my grade and every page I read is like listening to my grandmother's senile friend talk about her grandkids."

Relief flooded Bjorn. Kev had turned into one of the most reliable people he knew. They went downstairs and out to the parking lot where they piled into Kev's 1972 baby blue Nova. "Where to?"

"You see the crow over there?" asked Bjorn, pointing. "Follow the bird."

"No, let's not do this."

"Follow the bird."

"The last time I did that, a house burned down."

"And you saved three people from dying."

Kev sighed and pulled out of his parking spot. He turned left onto Wheeler and followed the crow as it flitted from perch to perch. "It's like the bird is waiting for us to follow," said Kev.

"Almost as if it is helping us," said Bjorn. "When we all know it does things for its own reasons that have nothing to do with me."

Kev turned to Bjorn. "Seriously, what is your problem with that bird?"

"It pecked me on the ear today," said Bjorn, pointing at the bloody organ. "It is not a nice bird."

Kev shook his head. "You're going to think I'm crazy, but all day I've had this feeling you were going to come and ask me to do something for you. And now you have! I know it's just a coincidence, but it doesn't feel like a coincidence. It feels like something I know for a fact. Do you know what I mean?"

"I do."

"I've also got this feeling you're in danger."

"I am sure you are correct."

"I mean like bear in the woods kind of danger. I can't shake the feeling."

"A bear is not in danger in the woods," said Bjorn.

"Why are you always so fucking difficult to talk to?"

The bird led them to a run-down part of midtown where frequent boarded up two and three-story buildings told the tale of inner city decline, and the only pedestrians were those who had no place to go to get off the streets.

"I think that is the destination," said Bjorn as he nodded toward a boarded up three-story brick façade building with a vacant drug store on the ground floor.

"Why doesn't your bird lead us to River Oaks or the best new taqueria or something like that? Why does he bring us to the worst shitholes?"

"Perhaps I need to have a conversation with him," said Bjorn, getting out of the car. "Park on the other side of the block until I get back. It may be safer if you are out of sight."

"What if you need help?"

"My father taught me many of the same things he taught Ivar. If I need help here, you can't provide it. Keep your windows rolled up."

"You think?"

Bjorn expected to have to break the glass to get through the door, but he checked it first and found it unlocked. A bell jingled as he slipped inside. Someone had been here. He found a used sleeping bag, some empty cans of food, and an overflowing ashtray, but no people. Bjorn noticed a hole in the ceiling, but nothing was visible in the dark space above. There were no stairs in the old drug store, so Bjorn exited and walked around the building. Around the side, he found an external set of stairs that led to a door with a missing door-knob. The door was ajar. Warily he stepped into the dark space and let his eyes adjust. Offices ringed the sides of the floor, but the whole center was a cubicle farm that formed a maze where anything could be hiding around any corner. The furniture was gone except for an occasional broken desk or chair. Bjorn made his way around the room looking into each cubicle as he passed. He turned a corner and saw the hole in the floor that he noticed when he was in the abandoned drug store.

"Don't turn around," whispered a voice behind him. "I have a gun."

Bjorn halted. He took a deep breath and slowly raised his

hands. When he exhaled, he let his breath go out like a thousand tendrils of his mind. His head felt cottony as his mind expanded. The figure behind him was dangerous, like any scared dog. Bjorn felt the man had a powerful connection to the elements. He could ooze through cracks, evaporate in the Sun, be absorbed into the Earth. Looked for, he was a vapor.

"I know you," said Bjorn. "Not your name, but I know you in your soul. You are like water, impossible to hold yet dangerous to those who are not careful. You are sneaky, treacherous, underhanded, and cowardly. But your words are just steam and bluster. If you had a gun you would have used it on me already."

"I do have a gun, asshole."

"Then you are out of bullets." Bjorn put down his hands and turned around. "You are no threat to me." Bjorn could sense the man's heartrate increase as panic set in. "Do not worry, wretch. I am not here to harm you. I came to help."

The man was scrawny and pale, thin lips surrounded by a blonde goatee, a knit cap over his golden curls, and a dirty turtleneck covering his thin frame. Even before Bjorn turned around, he knew from the man's accent this was a fellow Canadian.

"It's obvious you don't want to help me," said the man. "So who sent you? Who are you?"

"I don't understand why I'm here any more than you do," said Bjorn. "I'm just a pawn. My name doesn't matter. And neither does yours. I don't need to know who you are, so please don't tell me."

Just then, the bell on the pharmacy door jingled. The man moved cautiously around Bjorn so he could look down the hole.

"I wouldn't do that," said Bjorn.

The man waved him to silence. "It's safe. You can't see up here from down there. I watched you when you were downstairs and you had no idea I was here."

Bjorn heard measured footsteps in the drugstore under their feet. The footsteps stopped. Bjorn felt a sudden flash of panic and he reached out and pulled the man away from the hole. Gunfire erupted from below, three bullets passing through the hole and disappearing into the ceiling. Then Bjorn heard the sound of running.

"When he realizes there are no stairs in the pharmacy, it won't take him long to find the ones on the side of the building. We need to go out another way."

"There is no other way," said the man.

"There is always another way." Bjorn grabbed the man by the arm and dragged him to the back of the building. A window looked out across the roof of an adjacent building in the back.

"The windows don't open," said the man.

Bjorn threw a broken chair through the window then knocked out the broken shards that clung to the window frame.

"You want me to jump?" asked the man.

Bjorn grabbed him by the collar of his turtleneck and the back of his jeans and flung him out the window.

"Not necessary," said Bjorn, who jumped into a crouching position perched on the windowsill. From there he leaped down to the adjacent roof, landing like a cat. The other man lay on the roof like a discarded rag doll. Bjorn pulled him to his feet. The knit cap was gone, his blonde curls were tangled, and blood was running from his nose across his face. He groaned.

Bjorn led him across the roof of the shorter building until they were at the back of the block. Bjorn could see Kev's blue Nova parked nearby and the look of alarm as Kev noticed him. Kev buckled up and the engine came to life.

"Please don't throw me off this roof too!"

"Of course not," said Bjorn. "You'll jump down yourself."

"I don't know if I can."

"Lower yourself over the edge as far as you can and it won't be so bad. Like this." Bjorn turned around and lowered himself over the edge.

"Now you."

Reluctantly, the man followed Bjorn's example, casting glances back the way they had come. When they were both hanging by their hands, Bjorn let go and dropped the rest of the way to the sidewalk below. He bent his knees as he landed to minimize the jolt.

"Now you let go! Hurry up!" said Bjorn. "Your pursuer will be on us any second."

"Catch me!" said the man. He let go of the roof and fell to the sidewalk in a wrecked heap.

"Get up!" said Bjorn, but the man moved slowly, groaning as he went. Bjorn scooped him up and carried him to Kev's Nova where he slung him in the back seat. Bjorn slid into the front and buckled up. "Drive," he said, and Kev drove as if he were the getaway driver for a bank heist.

"Not so fast," said Bjorn. "You will draw attention to us."

"Where are we going?" asked Kev. Bjorn noticed his roommate's white knuckles on the driver's wheel.

"Anywhere, as long as it is far away."

"You fucked me up!" the man groaned from the back seat.

"Are you hungry? I know this crawfish place in Kemah," said Kev. "We're just getting into the season now and you've had nothing like it. It's more like food as an experience than meal, but not going to a dinner theater sort of experience, sort of cultural instead of entertainment, you know? Like, when you eat a burger—you don't have to pay attention to the burger and then a couple bites later it's all gone. But with crawfish you pay attention to what you're doing. You think about your food and it takes a long time to finish a plate of crawfish so the whole world has to go away for a while. It's meditation with calories."

"Sounds perfect," said Bjorn.

"I like crawfish," groaned the man in the backseat.

"Can you take us by back roads?" asked Bjorn.

They took 45 South out of Houston and Kev exited the freeway after they passed Hobby Airport. Thoroughfares and densely packed strip malls gave way to smaller roads and standalone buildings. Then there were corner stores and gas stations and small shops interspersed with empty lots and single-family homes. Soon they were driving through roads bounded by grassy flood plains dotted with scrubby pines and swamp oaks.

"Pull over here," Bjorn said when no human was in sight.

Kev flicked on his emergency lights and pulled off into a grassy patch.

"What's going on?" asked the man in the back. Bjorn didn't answer. He just got out of the car and opened the back door. The man began yelling and kicking when Bjorn reached for him, but Bjorn pulled him out of the car and tossed him into the field. Bjorn got back in the car and gestured for Kev to go. As Kev pulled back onto the road, Bjorn could hear the man yelling.

"I like crawfish too, you know!"

47

Bjorn did not know what to say. He did not know how he should feel. What he *did* feel was nausea mixed with emotions he had never expected to experience together: remorse, sadness, love, joy, anger, exhilaration, and even a groin-tightening lust. He had never felt so many emotions all at once. He was overwhelmed.

And on the other side of the door, he could feel Irina. Or maybe she wasn't there. He could also feel Anja —wherever she was— so his sense of proximity was all screwed up. His links to the two women were strong and confusing, like a pair of bright lights shining in his eyes. He scarcely knew where he ended and where they began, or which was which. He was in no state to have a conversation with either of them, but here he stood in front of Irina's door. He had to do something about the situation even if he wasn't up to it.

He knew he should knock. But if he knocked, Irina might not let him in, and this was hard enough as it was. He needed to get through it. She had given him a key to her room, which was surprising since they weren't allowed to have extra keys. Irina was resourceful like that, a quality he appreciated. If he let himself in, she might be angry at his intrusion, but would that make the situation worse than it already was?

Bjorn took the key out of his pocket. Better to barge in and have the conversation than be shut out. He turned the key in the lock and walked past the closet and into the room. He heard a low, sensual moan and felt a moment of horror. He might have walked in on Irina masturbating, which would explain the lust that came over him in front of Irina's door.

But that wasn't it. Instead, Bjorn saw Anja, her long, straight black hair disheveled and splayed out on the mattress like the rays of the Sun, her knees bent with Irina's head between her thighs. Bjorn realized that he had not been mixed up when he felt like both women were near him. Now he understood the flood of conflicting emotions and the intensity of his feelings.

For a moment, Bjorn stood there unnoticed. Then Anja turned her head and saw him. "What the fuck, Bjorn!"

"Oh, shit!" Irina said. "I forgot I gave him a key! This is super awkward, Bjorn. But… maybe a few years from now it will seem funny."

But Bjorn did not look at Irina. His eyes were locked on Anja's eyes. They blazed with the light of the sun. Her aura came into sharp focus. It was not a gentle color picked from a rainbow like most people's auras; it was like white fire radiating from a furnace. The radiance grew until it filled the room. Bjorn closed his eyes and still he saw the blinding light. Anger blasted him until he felt like a candle melting under a blowtorch. He sank to hands and knees and blindly moved toward the door.

"Bjorn, I know this is rough for you, but crawling away like a baby is ridiculous," said Irina. He heard her jump down from the top bunk and the shuffle of fabric against skin as she threw on some clothes.

Bjorn kept moving until he crossed the hallway and bumped into the wall. He turned around and sat with his back against it. He heard the soft barefoot padding of Irina following him and then the door closing. He could feel her strawberry lipstick breath on his face when she crouched down in front of him, but he could not see anything. His eyes were still dazzled by kaleidoscopic fractals of brilliant intensity.

Irina spoke into his blindness. "This is a hard way to find out. I get that. But this isn't the stoic response I was expecting. You need to man up a little here. You were an asshole to the two of us so you should be able to handle a little bit of poetic justice, don't you think?"

"I…"

"And yes, I suppose this did start out as a little bit of a revenge fuck as far as I was concerned but that disappeared overnight."

"It's only been a few nights."

"Exactly! This has happened like a whirlwind! It was the next thing to love at first sight, but it's the truest feeling I've ever had. Being with Anja is unlike anything I've experienced. I was wandering in the dark and now there's sunshine and warmth on my cheeks. You can't know what that's like."

"I know exactly what that's like," he croaked. "She is a goddess."

"What does that make me?" asked Irina, but her tone was light.

"No, no. I think she is divine. She is an incarnation of a goddess on Earth."

"Nevermind, I'm not really offended," said Irina. "I know what you mean. I'm totally in love with Anja too, only I would never do to her what you did to us. But I don't want you to think I'm still mad at you. If you weren't a secret jackass I would never have met the love of my life. She is worth living for. On top of that, this will crush my mom's hopes for me. I can't wait to introduce them and watch mom's plastic face crumble. And that's all because of you. I guess you were not the mistake I was waiting to make."

Bjorn's vision was clearing. He saw Irina take the key out of his hand then stand up and go back to her room. The door closed behind her, the lock clicked, and he was alone.

"I was not your mistake to regret," he whispered, "But you were mine."

48

Becky sat on the floor with her legs tucked up against her body and her voluminous orange t-shirt pulled over her legs and feet so only her toes poked out from the bottom. "If you don't put out, Unfrid, I'm going to ask you to leave," she said. "And by 'put out' I mean put more effort into this game. I know I'm going to beat you but please, please make this as challenging as you can!"

As an RA, Becky had a room to herself. The furniture was the same as everyone else's, but her posters were blueprints of an Apollo rocket, a Soyuz, and a space shuttle. An orrery clock radio sat on the bedside table.

"I'm not sure I'm in the right frame of mind to put up the fight you crave."

"Then why don't you tell me what's bothering you? I'm your RA and I'm here for you. I'm like a bartender who won't let you drink any alcohol."

"We could do some weed."

"Shut up!" she said with a laugh. "That never happened! Now spill; what's bothering you?"

Bjorn couldn't explain what happened between him, Anja, and Irina. Even if he were in a frame of mind to talk about it, she wouldn't believe it. But there were other things on his mind.

"I met a Helgrind," Bjorn said.

"A what? Is that like haggis?"

"No, haggis is a disgusting Scottish food. A Helgrind is a human so afraid of death that they will make desperate deals with the goddess of the underworld to preserve their life. That goddess is called Hel. In Old Scandinavian the Helgrind was a grave, the door to Hel's underworld. When we use the word 'Helgrind' for a person in modern Norse, it is someone who stands at the door to the underworld but will not go in."

"It's like… making a deal with the Devil? You sell your soul?"

Bjorn shrugged. "The dead already belong to Hel, so the Helgrind has nothing to sell. They are bartering service on Earth for a little more time. The Christian idea is more black and white than the Viking idea."

"Bartering with the lord of the underworld sounds black and white to me."

"In our way of thinking, good and evil are not absolutes. What is good for one person is evil for another."

"Murder is evil."

"Not in self-defense. Not to protect your country or your family."

"That's not considered murder."

"The person being killed still thinks it's murder. You see? Evil for one person is good for another."

"Eating babies," said Becky. "Eating babies is pure evil."

"But they are delicious!" said Bjorn.

In retaliation, Becky jumped four of his pieces, ended the game, and told him to get out. But when he went to leave, she grabbed his arm and made him sit down again. She kept him there talking until late into the night when his grief had subsided to a dull ache.

49

Bjorn lay on his bunk picking out words he recognized from a Russian language edition of *A Canticle for Leibowitz*. He was trying to find a way to study on his own that did not put him to sleep. He already knew what Miller was trying to say in the book, and that was half the battle. At least it was not boring.

Kev sat at his desk with his back to Bjorn, working on his big history research project.

When the Crone appeared in the room, Bjorn flinched, fumbled his book and nearly dropped it.

He sat up and rolled his eyes at the spirit.

"Bjorn Unfrid," said the Crone. "It is true you saved the endangered one, but his death was merely delayed. To fulfill the bargain he must be delivered out of danger altogether. Your task is not yet complete."

Bjorn shrugged. Must he save everyone?

"I know you don't want to do this. Your reluctance will only grow. Promise me you will do what is necessary to complete the bargain."

Bjorn shrugged.

"Speak the words," she said.

Bjorn pointed at Kev's back. He wasn't going to have a conversation with the Crone that would make his roommate think he was schizophrenic.

The Crone looked at Kev and then rolled her own eyes. She put her hands on her hips in exasperation as he had seen his own mother do countless times. Mostly the Crone spoke as formally as Bjorn, but just now it was like he was seeing an actor in between takes talking out of character. If he had not been so angry at the Crone for all the ways she had messed up his life, he might have found her endearing.

"Forget about your roommate," the Crone said. "Just promise me you'll do what needs to be done."

Bjorn wrote on his notebook next to all the scribbled post-apocalyptic Russian words, *I will do it and get it over with and then we are done. As far I am concerned, this has already taken too long!!!!* Then he turned the notebook around so she could see his words.

"I receive your promise," said the Crone. "And don't be concerned that this process is drawn out. A road trip can take days or weeks but it can finish with a crash and be over in seconds. Soon, Bjorn, you will be on the other side of it all and it will seem like it came to an end too abruptly."

Bjorn frowned at the Crone. In his notebook he wrote *What do you mean by other side? What is wrong with you?* But when he turned the notebook around so she could read it, the Crone was gone.

50

Bjorn was thinking about the Crone's cryptic words a few days later when Ivar knocked on his door. "Nothing fancy tonight," said Bjorn's brother. He was dressed in a pair of jeans with a button-down long-sleeved shirt and a light jacket. The brothers went downstairs and out to the parking lot. Ivar stopped in front of his black rental car. "Just what we needed," he said. "An omen."

A crow walked back and forth on the hood of the car.

"I am not sure they are really omens," said Bjorn. "Maybe they are just everywhere and when things happen people say 'Oh, there was a crow. It was an omen.'"

Ivar leaned over the hood and tried to shoo the bird away. It hopped out of reach and cawed angrily but stayed on the car.

"I don't know," said Ivar. "It doesn't want to leave when I shoo it away. That doesn't seem like normal crow behavior. It's what I expect out of an omen, though. Just can't tell if it's good or bad."

Bjorn leaned over the hood until he was face to face with the bird. "That's why a crow omen is useless! It's good for one person and bad for the other and you can't tell how it's going to turn out until it happens. Totally useless!"

The crow cawed angrily at him.

"Do you know this bird?" asked Ivar.

"Can we just go?"

They got in the car and Ivar pulled out of the parking spot. "The crow isn't an omen because it predicts the future," said Ivar. "It's because the crow is always watching. It knows where the turning points will be and it observes. Omens aren't about foretelling the future. They're about knowing where the crossroads are."

"You think dinner will be a turning point for us?" asked Bjorn. "Maybe that's what the crow wanted to observe."

His brother shrugged. "House Unfrid is more consequential than you know. What we do affects people far away from the neighborhoods we come from. It's been like that for generations. Every choice you and I make could change things for people around us."

"If I order salad, will the beef industry fall?"

"You are a pouty shit tonight, *brodir*. What the fuck is up with you?"

Bjorn side eyed his older brother. "You admitted you perceive the spirit world. How well do you perceive it?"

"Mostly through smell. But that's a lot better than it sounds. In your room I could tell there was some awful shit under your bed. I don't know what you were fucking with."

"That was my roommate's mess. The house that burned down? That was when I confronted the spirit there."

"I can smell women on you, too. With the scent of heartbreak mixed in. I've been waiting for you to tell me what's going on there. And there's other things too. There's a powerful woodland spirit around here somewhere. I get the scent of northern pines and wild animals. I was wondering if it was following you."

"Definitely not following me. That's a Manitou."

"There's other Major Arcana hovering in your sphere as well," said Ivar. "I'm guessing you can sense them too?"

"I can see them."

Ivar's eyebrows went up. "Major Arcana revealed themselves to you? They chose you?"

Bjorn shook his head. "I see them all the time. I can have conversations with them too. Ghosts and lesser spirits I can tune out and ignore most of the time, but the Arcana I always see as clearly as I see you."

"That is… that is huge…"

"They're assholes," said Bjorn. "Not intentionally maybe, but all they care about is their mission or sphere or whatever it is. They don't tell you what's really going on or what they know."

Ivar burst out laughing. "You can't honestly tell me that bothers you, can you? You of all people? You honor Loki. Loki doesn't tell his left foot where his right foot is walking."

"I'm not devout…"

"Well, who is these days? But really, you like the trickster so much."

"But he's also the most honest, the one who speaks the truth no one wants to hear."

"And doesn't it strike you that the most brutally honest one among the Asgardian Arcana enjoys fooling people? And let me be blunt here; honesty is overrated. Look where being honest gets Loki. Everyone thinks he's an asshole and a bad guy because he's so honest. And guess what? It's true. Honest people can be the biggest assholes of all."

"I think a lot of Loki's reputation as a bad guy in popular culture comes from getting Baldur killed."

"Yeah, that didn't help him out either," said Ivar.

Bjorn digested Ivar's words for a few moments. "Are you defending the Arcana's behavior?" he asked.

"I'm just saying that if you can see the Arcana the way you say, you have to remember they will never be as forthcoming with you as you are with everyone else. Unless you want to go the route of a priest to one of them? I don't see you doing that, though."

"Definitely not!"

"Then it's the path of the mage, and mages are on their own. Sooner or later you'll deal with an Arcana when you shouldn't have, probably sooner."

Bjorn pressed his lips into a grim line, but Ivar was watching the road and did not seem to notice.

"Oh, wait! You're not totally alone!" said Ivar with a laugh. "You've got that crow!"

Ivar pulled into the parking lot of a Tex Mex joint with stucco façade and earthy green and red colors. They ate fresh bowls of hot corn chips while they waited for their fajitas. Ivar's eyes watered from the salsa and he had to wipe his nose as it ran.

"This is good shit!" Ivar said hoarsely.

"I am possessed by a fire Arcana!" said Bjorn as he wiped his brow with a napkin. He nodded to a nearby couple who gave him strange looks at his words.

When the brothers finished eating, they left the restaurant laughing and joking. Streetlamps and the bright colors of glowing retail signs broke the darkness of the chilly night. The sounds of freeway traffic and the smell of beans and salsa surrounded them. Both men fell abruptly silent as they stepped into the parking lot, their cheer replaced with foreboding.

"Fuck!" said Ivar.

Ivar's car was covered with dozens of crows crowded together on the hood, the roof, and the trunk. The birds jostled each other trying not to be pushed off the edge by the other birds. No other car in the parking lot had a single bird perched on it.

"The crow is always like this," said Bjorn. "He's very dramatic. Apparently they all are."

"This isn't a joking matter anymore," said Ivar. "This is a real warning."

"To do what?" asked Bjorn. "Or is it not to do something? Do you have an instruction booklet for crow omens? What can I do but go on the same way?"

Ivar sighed. "I see what you mean. Come on, I need to take you somewhere and show you something." The brothers got in the car. The birds did not scatter until the car pulled into traffic. "What makes you so important, Bjorn?"

"Nothing."

"What's your connection to those birds?"

Bjorn sighed. "The crow is my spirit animal. That is the only special thing I can think of."

"My spirit animal is the wolf."

"Ah!" said Bjorn. "Wolves are cool!"

"Yeah, but a wolf pack has never come to guide me the way those crows come to you. What's been going on since you left Toronto?"

While Ivar drove, Bjorn told his brother about following Anja to Houston, the shadow of doom hanging over Irina, how he met the Crone, and the first semester Russian final exam.

"No shit!" said Ivar. "Say something in Russian."

"*Tvoy bespokoynyy prizrak budet khodit' po miru,*" said Bjorn.

Ivar laughed. "No way! An Arcana taught you a language. What did you say?"

Bjorn opened his mouth to speak but said nothing.

"What? What's up with you?"

"I don't know what I said. The words just came to me."

"You are a spooky little shit, *brodir,*" said Ivar. "Is that everything?"

Bjorn shook his head. He told Ivar about the lamprey spirit and his attempts to save Kev from it. He told about the night the house burned down. As he finished speaking, Ivar pulled into a parking lot for a rundown warehouse. "We're here," said Ivar.

"Do you want me to tell you what the Crone asked me to do?" asked Bjorn.

"After. Let's go in."

"This looks like someplace the crow would lead me," Bjorn said.

"Abandoned places have always been my natural element," said Ivar. "No people, no rules."

"But there are rules everywhere. And laws."

"Trust me, when people are not around, the only rules are the ones you keep in your mind. These are the places I go to feel free. These are the places I work." Ivar opened the trunk and retrieved a small suitcase before leading Bjorn to the front door. Ivar stepped over a broken padlock, opened the door and entered the warehouse. Inside the cavernous room, moonlight streamed through the large, high windows and projected squares of light on the concrete floor. A rusted barrel sat squarely in the light. Ivar strode directly to it. He set down the suitcase and took a lighter out of his pocket, which he used to light wadded up newspapers in the barrel. Soon there was a cheerful fire.

"What are you burning?"

"There were some pallets left in the corner. I've been going through one or two per night."

"Why here? How many nights?"

"I followed a scent. That's how I operate. Maybe it's not a scent in the real world. It can be a scent from the spirit world. It can be a premonition too. Sometimes it comes to me before there's anything to smell. Sometimes it's a puzzle I have to figure out. This one has kept me coming back, but now I've got it figured out."

Ivar opened the suitcase. The inside was filled with foam with cutouts to fit bottles, glasses, and small miscellaneous containers. "This is my portable bar," said Ivar as he retrieved several bottles and stood them up on the cement floor. He took out a pair of tumblers and a small thermos, which he opened. Ice clinked from the thermos to the tumblers.

"None for me, thanks," said Bjorn.

"I know you're no stranger to hard liquor," said Ivar.

"I usually only drink for special occasions."

"I'm leaving tomorrow," said Ivar as he opened the various bottles and mixed the contents of the tumblers. In the flickering light of the burn barrel, Ivar's hands seemed to dance with the quick sleights of a magician's fingers.

"You are an alchemist!" said Bjorn.

"Taste that and you will realize how true your words are," he said as he handed over one of the tumblers.

Bjorn sipped the contents. The liquid tasted light and fruity at first, but as it moved down his throat it changed to a whisky burn that was smooth and buttery. "Oh my Gods!" said Bjorn. "I've never heard of something like this. What do you call it?"

"It's the Atomic Hangover."

"I don't like the name at all. I hope it doesn't live up to it."

Ivar laughed. "Oh it does, it does! But it's worth it. Drink it down. Now tell me more about the Crone."

Bjorn took a deep drink from the tumbler and told his brother about his connection to Irina and the high price he would have to pay to save her. All around the distant walls danced the shadows cast by the burn barrel's flames. They moved around and around the fire like a tribe in the moonlight. He could hear a far-off drum and voices of the People calling to their Manitous.

"This is the strongest drink I think I've ever had," said Bjorn, who could feel himself grinning but could do nothing to stop it. "I'm only half here. I'm not sure where the other half is."

"Tell me the rest of the story about the Crone," said Ivar.

"No, later. I want to hear about the smell that led you to this warehouse."

"Okay. It's the smell of the grave, like fresh-turned earth. It's death but also renewal. Everything that dies is reborn again, first in worms and then in growing shoots and budding flowers, in ripe fruit, and then in a living animal and maybe again in a human. It's how I keep a positive outlook. The grave scent invigorates me."

"If I killed as many people as you, I would want to look on the bright side too. All I smell is concrete and smoke though."

"That's why it's my gift and not yours, Bjorn. It's also not as straightforward as your Sight. I've had to figure out what things mean. It's like learning to read Runes or Tarot."

"And the grave means rebirth."

"To me. But the reason the scent is here is because it is the spoor of Hel. One who belongs to the death goddess is destined to come here. I figure he has begged her for his life, which is why her smell is on him. I think she granted his request because so far he has managed to escape me when his partners could not. There were seven of them just a few weeks ago but he is the last. If not for Hel looking out for him, I would be home in Toronto already."

The grin slid off Bjorn's face. "I met a Helgrind," he said.

"I know you did Bjorn, I know you did. I knew your scent in the drug store."

"I think I need to finish this drink," said Bjorn, tipping the tumbler and draining it.

"Me too," said Ivar, draining his glass as well.

When they finished their drinks, Bjorn looked into Ivar's eyes. The shifting light from the fire made them alternate between hard, glittering stars and deep wells of shadow.

"Now tell me, little brother, what business did you have harboring a Helgrind?"

"The Crone demands payment for her help. I am the surety of the Helgrind's safety."

"His name is Olaf," said Ivar. "The Helgrind, that is. I am oathbound to be his doom."

Bjorn shivered. "'Oathbound'. When did you start using words like that?"

Ivar smiled. "Would you prefer me to say I promised to kill the fucker?"

"How important is that promise to you?" asked Bjorn.

"I've never broken a promise. I never will break a promise. How important is your debt to the Crone?"

"It's Karma."

"You're not Hindu," said Ivar.

"Call it destiny then or whatever you like. I am bound to it. This is so fucked up and wrong! I cannot believe this is happening."

"The Arcana know what they're doing, Bjorn. Anyone else in this city who tried to come between me and my mark would be dead already."

"I think I need another drink," said Bjorn.

"Yeah, me too," said Ivar. He took Bjorn's tumbler and mixed them each another drink. "Our situations are not symmetrical, however," he said.

"What do you mean?"

"I mean that while we are each bound to our task, we are in different positions."

"I don't understand," said Bjorn. "It's the same for both of us."

Ivar handed Bjorn's tumbler back to him. "You might understand if you didn't have an Atomic Hangover futzing with your brain. I'll explain. The only way for you to succeed in protecting your weaselly friend…"

"Not my friend," said Bjorn, swaying slightly and feeling loose. "In fact, I could come to hate him with only the tiniest effort on my part. He is at best an unpleasant chore."

"Okay, then, the only way to succeed at your unpleasant chore is to kill me because I will not stop until I have murdered him. I am in a different position from you, however. I don't need to kill you. I only need a few seconds with Olaf to complete my task. Then we are both free and alive and you and I can go back to the way things were."

"Could we really go back to the way things were though?"

"Totally. I can always forgive and forget your mistakes as long as I get what I want."

"That is very big of you."

"It is, isn't it?"

"Are you familiar with irony?"

"The sticky spot I see," said Ivar, ignoring Bjorn's comment, "is intent. I wouldn't complain if you just let me kill Olaf, but I don't think that would satisfy your debt to the Crone. You have to try to kill me for real. The bad part about that is if you did, I would have to kill you and then I would be put out of the family. Dad would be obligated to do it. My protection would end and all the enemies of House Unfrid would come after me because killing me would hurt Dad. Hell, some of our allies would come after us too. We're not exactly a popular family, even with our 'friends' in the industry."

"I hate the family business," said Bjorn.

"It's got its drawbacks," said Ivar. "But it has its advantages, too."

"So we don't have any way out," said Bjorn.

"Of course we do!" said Ivar. "You're going to try to kill me tonight, little brother. I just have to get the better of you without killing you and then find Olaf and snap him like a twig. Then we're both free."

The Crone stepped out of a shadowy corner of the room. "You must kill him now," she said. "You have little time."

"Grafimide! Fragricide! I mean fratricide!" said Bjorn. "I'm a little tongue-tied but you are... You are a bitch, an Arcade of bitches."

"I think you mean 'Arcana of bitches'," said Ivar.

"Thank you. That's exactly what I was meaning when I said that. An arcade is fun, but an Arcana is not and that's what I was getting at. Odin's balls I'm drunk! What was I saying?"

"I think you were confronting the Crone about bargaining for you to kill your own brother. I know she's here. She smells like potpourri and old ladies."

"Probably. That sounds right. Both about killing and also the old lady thing," said Bjorn, his tongue feeling thick and awkward.

"She's a little slow," said Ivar. "The Arcana often are. Has she warned you yet that you must be quick about your business?"

"Murder is murder regardless of the relations involved," said the Crone, "and humans are murderers. Your hands are all red, and working with humans is a bloody business. You have come to the part where you just need to get it done, Bjorn. Do what you must."

"She's conceptualizing," said Bjorn.

"I don't think so," said Ivar.

"Mitigating?"

"Probably not," said Ivar.

"Rationalizing."

"That sounds like it might be right."

"I can ham barely talk," said Bjorn.

"The Atomic Hangover is a powerful drink," said Ivar. "I'm impressed you're still talking at all."

"You sound fine."

"I was drinking mineral water with lemon."

Bjorn's shoulders slumped and he looked down at the glass in his hand. "I'mma drug too, right?"

"Big time. The sedatives are what gives you the hangover

in the morning. They wouldn't if they weren't mixed with alcohol, but I figured you should have some fun. You're still just a kid."

"You must kill him now," said the Crone. "Honor your agreement!"

"Fuck it," said Bjorn, tossing his glass away. It shattered on the concrete. "Gotta try while I'mma stand."

"Oh, we're doing this now, eh?" asked Ivar. He tossed his glass away as well before taking up a low stance with his feet wide. "Okay, I'm ready!"

Bjorn charged his brother and locked arms with him. Ivar retreated a step so Bjorn lurched forward off balance. Ivar used the opportunity to twist his brother around and lock him up from behind.

"There we go," said Ivar. "I'll hold you here a few minutes, you will go to sleep and then it will be all over."

But Bjorn strained against his brother's hold, slowly prying Ivar's arms out of place until he was free. He skittered away and turned to face Ivar. Both men were panting with the exertion.

"You are a helluva lot stronger than the last time we wrestled," said Ivar.

"I was fishteen," said Bjorn.

"And you still smell like a fish," said Ivar with a laugh. He lunged at Bjorn, but stopped when Bjorn punched him in the face.

"Really?"

"Ha!" said Bjorn, "you weren't expectorating that."

Ivar lunged again, grabbed his brother, and pulled him to the ground, his legs locked around Bjorn's waist and his arms immobilized him in a full Nelson.

"Ugh," said Bjorn. "I can't move."

"Right now I prefer you like that," said Ivar.

Bjorn strained against Ivar's hold but could not get out. He lay on the concrete defeated and overpowered.

"Tricked me," said Bjorn, "and I'm the Loki guy. Totally stole my thunder."

"Like I said, you're a kid. And you are not a trickster, Bjorn."

"I thought of a trick," said Bjorn, "It's the most cool but I cannima na move hamma do it."

"What?" said Ivar. "Never mind. Just be patient and relax and you can sleep it off. Everything will be fine in the morning."

Then there came the sound of something hitting one of the high windows. Locked together, the brothers could barely turn their heads enough to see the windows. Impact after impact jolted the glass.

"That's birds crashing into the window," said Ivar. The impacts came faster and faster. "That's a lot of dead birds," said Ivar. "I don't think I like this."

The sound of the birds striking the window grew into a continuous hail. The birds blotted out the light of the moon. Cracks appeared in the window and finally the glass burst inward and scores of crows flew through the opening, spreading across the warehouse. The birds dove at Ivar's face. Bjorn could feel his brother's grip loosen.

"Just hold on," said Bjorn, but Ivar let him go to ward off the avian swarm.

Bjorn levered himself up to his hands and knees. Ivar was covered with crows like a cookie swarmed with ants. "Shit," he said. The birds scattered and cawed as Bjorn plunged his hands into the mass. He straddled his brother and his hands closed around Ivar's throat. He pushed down with his full weight. Ivar grabbed at Bjorn's wrists but could not pry his grip loose.

"Finish him!" urged the Crone.

Nothing felt real to Bjorn. His fingers were white from fierce effort, but he knew that Ivar would turn the tables any moment. Ivar's fingers pushed and pulled, struck Bjorn in the side of the head, but Bjorn felt nothing. Ivar's face turned red and his eyes bulged.

"Don't worry! I tol' you I got this trick, a real Loki trick" whispered Bjorn. "I can do it too. I can. You'll see. You'll see. You're the best brother. I would never let you down. I love you. I think the Nuclear Hangover is making me weepy."

Ivar's eyes glazed over and his hands stopped moving. The Crone stood by Bjorn's side.

Bjorn's eyes ran with tears. "Are we square, Crone?" he asked. "Is the debt paid?"

"It is paid," she said. And then she was gone.

"Now it is time for the Loki shit," Bjorn said, moving off Ivar's body. "We'll see how the Crone likes this trick." He stuck his finger down Ivar's throat to make sure the passage was open, then he knelt beside him. One hand behind the other, he interlaced his fingers and began chest compressions.

"One... two... three... four..." he counted. He put one hand under Ivar's neck to straighten the air passage, then held the nose closed and puffed into Ivar's mouth. He went back to chest compressions and counted again. He repeated the cycle.

Bjorn's mind was foggy and he had to concentrate on the numbers. Did he just say three? Or was it two? He did not feel entirely in his own head. Chest compressions. The murder of crows flew away until only one remained. It cawed each time he pushed down on Ivar's chest.

Soon, Bjorn was doing the whole routine by feel. The lights had gone out or the fire had died down. He could see nothing. No, that made no sense. His eyes must be closed. He used to know how to open them. There must be a way.

"One... two... three... four..."

Bjorn hoped he was doing compressions on Ivar's chest and not someplace else.

What if he wasn't doing compressions at all? He floated, detached, no longer a part of the physical world.

Bjorn's mind dwindled like a flame going out, but before consciousness was completely gone, light came to him again and his thoughts began to clear. He was abruptly lucid and sober. Bjorn stood on the concrete floor but everything seemed much bigger, towering over him. On the floor nearby he could see Ivar's body. He could also see his own body slumped over his brother.

He was having an out of body experience.

No he wasn't. He definitely had a body.

Panicked, Bjorn hopped and fluttered and then he was aloft, flying around the warehouse. He was inside the crow. Bjorn landed on Ivar's chest, next to his own face.

He had to wake up and start the chest compressions again. Bjorn willed himself back into his own body but nothing happened. He hopped from foot to foot. If he could not will himself back where he belonged, then he had to force his body to wake up.

He pecked his cheek. He felt nothing and there was no response. He pecked harder and harder and harder until blood oozed across Ivar's chest. He jumped on his own head and pecked his scalp but nothing happened. Bjorn could taste the blood on the crow's tongue.

If he would just wake up everything would be fine.

Bjorn pecked faster and faster, turning his hair red. He grew angrier and angrier knowing that time was running out.

He was *right here*! All he had to do was get up! He pecked savagely at the most tender spots of the face. A poke in the eye would surely break through the drug-induced sleep, but it didn't. Bjorn poked again, biting in anger that only grew with his desperation. He bit as hard as he could and yanked to make it as painful as possible.

The eye came free, a white marble with a brown iris muddied by blood and held between the black pincers of his beak, yet he still did not wake up. In a rage, Bjorn swallowed the eye.

He left the two bodies then, flying through the broken window. He flew until the sun came up. He climbed as high as he could, but the sun would not burn him to ash. He flew until he could fly no more. Exhausted, Bjorn alighted and immediately went to sleep.

When he awoke, excruciating pain radiated from his eye socket. Bjorn's head pounded with the aftereffects of the drugs in his system, and the wounds across his face felt like razorblades in the frosty air. But worst of all, his brother was as cold as the concrete floor. Bjorn stood stiffly and staggered out the front door in a blue-sky dawn that did not know to weep for his fate. He had to call their mother and confess what had happened.

As he walked, he heard cawing all around him. Crows gathered on lampposts and fences, on the branches of trees and the edges of buildings. They filled every high perch. They cawed like fans chanting at a football game, but it was not random noise to Bjorn's ears anymore. He heard them like a person remembering a forgotten language. The meaning of their calls was clear.

Hail Lord Crow! Hail Lord Crow! Hail Lord Crow!

Thank you!

Dear Reader,

Writing about Bjorn and his friends was a lot of fun and very rewarding, but even better is knowing that you read this and that it mattered to you. If this book moved you in some way, please support Bjorn and future works in his world by leaving a review for *The Saga of Bjorn Unfrid* on Goodreads or other online platforms. And if you haven't visited our website, please drop by to see us at RinthPress.net.

Thank you so much for coming on this journey with us!

John L. Simons Jr.

About the Author

John Simons spun wild stories and considered himself a writer from childhood, even when the world knew him only as a teacher, retailer, business consultant, or founder of a comic convention. Right now he is likely learning a language, thinking about fish or dinosaurs, moaning about how his garden doesn't produce tomatoes, serving the canines who run the house, or fighting off his kids, who think his love of martial arts is a reason to attack him whenever he is not expecting it. It probably is.